P9-CQK-282

DEAR DUMB DIARY,

A TRIPLE SCOOP OF RAGE WITH GIGGLE SPRINKLES

BOOKS #1–3

BY JAMIE KELLY

SCHOLASTIC INC.

New York Toronto London Auckland
Sydney Mexico City New Delhi Hong Kong

Dear Dumb Diary #1: Let's Pretend This Never Happened,
ISBN 978-0-439-62904-1, copyright © 2004 by Jim Benton.

Dear Dumb Diary #2: My Pants Are Haunted!,
ISBN 978-0-439-62905-8, copyright © 2004 by Jim Benton.

Dear Dumb Diary #3: Am I the Princess or the Frog?,
ISBN 978-0-439-62907-2, copyright © 2005 by Jim Benton.

The books were originally published by Apple Paperbacks.

ISBN 978-0-545-08837-4

17 16 15 14 13 12   17 18 19 20/0
Printed in the U.S.A.   40
This collection first printing, May 2008

This special
TRIPLE SCOOP OF RAGE
WITH GIGGLE SPRINKLES
includes these three Jamie Kelly diaries:

This DIARY PROPERTY OF

Jamie Kelly

SCHOOL: MACKEREL MIDDLE SCHOOL

LOCKER: 101

BEST FRIEND: Isabella

PET: Stinker which is a beagle

EYE COLOR: Green

HAIR COLOR: ~~BROWN~~ Brownishly Blond with Brunette Brownness

The Last Person Who Kept Reading →

THIS IS NOT
YOUR DIARY

I CAN TELL

Dear Whoever Is Reading My Dumb Diary,

Are you sure you're supposed to be reading somebody else's diary? Maybe I told you that you could, so that's okay. But if you are Angeline, I did NOT give you permission, so stop it.

If you are my parents, then YES, I know that I am not allowed to call people idiots and fools and goons and halfwits and pinheads and all that, but this is a diary, and I didn't actually "call" them anything. I *wrote* it. And if you punish me for it, then I will know that you read my diary, which I am *not* giving you permission to do.

Now, by the power vested in me, I do promise that everything in this diary is true or, at least, as true as I think it needs to be.

Signed,

Jamie Kelly

PS: If this is you, Angeline, reading this, then HA-HA! I got you! For I have written this in poison ink on a special poison paper, and you had better run and call 911 right now!

PSS: If this is you, Hudson, reading this, I have an antidote to the poison and it is conveniently available to you through a simple phone call to my house. But don't mention the poison thing to my parents if they answer. I think they might be all weird about me poisoning people.

Here they ARE
DiSAPPROVING POISONING

Monday 02

Dear Dumb Diary,

   I was out playing with my beagle, Stinker, this afternoon and I was doing that thing where you pretend to throw the ball and then don't throw it and Stinker starts running for it until he realizes you didn't really throw it at all. Usually I only do it two or three times but today I guess I was thinking about something else, because when I finally realized that I hadn't thrown the ball yet, I had probably done it about a hundred and forty times. Stinker was a little bit cross-eyed and foamy and he wouldn't come back in the house for a long time.
   I wonder if dogs can hold a grudge.

Frustration Foam

Tuesday 03

Dear Dumb Diary,

I think I was very nearly *nicknamed* today, which is almost the worst thing that can happen to you in middle school. I was eating a peach at lunch and another peach fell out of my bag onto the floor, and Mike Pinsetti, who only breathes through his mouth, was standing there and he said, "Hey, Peach Girl."

He's pretty much the official nicknamer of the school, and Pinsetti's labels, although stupid, often stick. (Don't believe me, Diary? Just ask old "Butt Buttlington," who was one of Pinsetti's very first nicknames. I don't even know his real name. Nobody does. He's been called Butt Buttlington for so long that his mom actually called him Butt by accident one time when she dropped him off at school. "Bye, Butt Buttlington," she said. Then when she realized what she had done, she tried to make it better by following up with: "We're proud of you.")

One second Before You Get A Nickname

One Second After You Get A Nickname

Back to my peach story. I picked the backstabbing fruit up real quick. I thought nobody had heard Pinsetti, which pretty much cancels out a nickname. But then this adorable musical laughter that sounds like somebody is tickling a baby by rubbing its tummy with a puppy comes from behind me. When I turn around, I see it's none other than Angeline, who was probably evilly committing this nickname to memory.

It's only a matter of time before I have to start signing my homework as **PEACH GIRL**.

Wednesday 04

Dear Dumb Diary,

Today Hudson Rivers (eighth cutest guy in my grade) talked to me in the hall. Normally, this would have no effect on me at all, since there is still a chance that Cute Guys One Through Seven might actually talk to me one day. But when Hudson said, "Hey," today, I could tell that he was totally in love with me, and I felt that I had an obligation to be irresistible for his benefit.

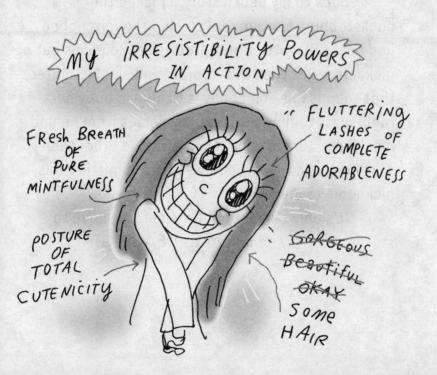

MY IRRESISTIBILITY POWERS IN ACTION

FLUTTERING LASHES OF COMPLETE ADORABLENESS

FRESH BREATH OF PURE MINTFULNESS

POSTURE OF TOTAL CUTENICITY

~~GORGEOUS~~
~~BEAUTIFUL~~
~~OKAY~~
SOME HAIR

So just as I'm about to say something cool back to Hudson (Maybe even something REALLY cool. We'll never know for sure now.), Angeline comes around the corner with her jillion cute things dangling from her backpack, and intentionally looks cute RIGHT IN FRONT OF HIS EYES. This scorpion-like behavior on her part made me forget what I was going to say, so the only thing that came out of my mouth was a gush of air without any words in it. Not like this mattered, because he was staring at Angeline the same way Stinker was staring at the ball a couple days ago.

STINKER   HUDSON

It was pretty obvious that all of his love for me was squirting out his ears all over the floor. Ask Isabella if you don't believe me. She was standing right there.

As if that wasn't vicious enough, get this:

He says to Angeline: "Wow, is that your Lip Smacker I smell? ChocoMint? It's great."

Angeline stops for just a second and **LOOKS RIGHT AT ISABELLA AND ME.** Then she says to Hudson, "Yeah, it is." And her radiant smile freezes him in his tracks.

Frankly, I think that it is just rude and obscene to have teeth white enough to hurt and maybe **PERMANENTLY DAMAGE** the eyes of onlookers.

(In case my children are reading this years from now, this is the exact moment Angeline stole your father, Hudson, from me, and it is her fault that now your last name is Rumpelstiltskin or Schwarzenegger or Buttlington.)

SAD SAD FUTURE BABY LEARNing that his father has been STOLEN

DUMB DIARY

Angeline's fault

Here's the thing: Isabella is the **ONLY** girl in the entire school who uses ChocoMint Lip Smacker. It's the grossest flavor they ever made, but she **needed** her very own unique Lip Smacker flavor, and so she settled on the only one nobody else likes. All the girls know it's hers. Even Angeline knows it.

So Dumb Diary, let's see that scene again in slow motion: Suddenly, in one swift move, Angeline had stolen my future prom date/boyfriend/ husband, and Isabella had lost her signature Lip Smacker scent. (Isabella would rather wear her grandma's giant-bottomed pants to school than let anyone think she is copying Angeline.)

A MYSTERY of NATURE

ISABELLA'S HUMAN- SIZED BUTT

ISABELLA'S GRANDMA'S HORSE-LIKE BUTT

I suppose I could have said something, but I knew that Angeline had the "Peach Girl" nickname loaded in her Imaginary Slingshot of Pure Wickedness and was ready to let me have it right in front of Hudson.

I was powerless.

Of course, Dumb Diary, you understand that I'm **DESTROYED**. What you may not fully appreciate is the impact this scandalous event is having on Isabella. She is **EXTREMELY** smell-oriented, and not really well-equipped to change her scented ointments. I foresee a long, painful bout with chapped lips in her future.

It also occurs to me, Dumb Diary, that Angeline is so perfect that the word "perfect" is probably not perfect enough for her. One day they'll have to invent another word for her and when they do I hope it rhymes with vomit or turd because I think I have a good idea for a song if they do.

PRINCESS TURD OF TURDSYLVANIA

Wednesday, The Evening Edition

Dear Dumb Diary,

    Tonight at dinner, Mom announced that we're going to be taking care of my little cousin in a few weeks. He's, like, my aunt's daughter's brother's nephew or something.

    I know that your uncle's kids are your cousins, but then there are things like first cousins and second cousins and cousins once-removed. What does that mean? "Cousins once-removed."

    I had a wart once removed.

cousin
once-removed

wart
once removed

And, Dumb Diary, just to update you on Mom's Latest Food-Crime, last night she made a casserole with 147 ingredients, and it still tasted bad. It's hard to believe that out of 147 ingredients, not one of them tasted good.

Of course I ate it anyway. If you don't eat it, Mom gives you the speech on hard work and how the hungry children in Wheretheheckistan would just love her casserole.

It seems to me the kids in Wheretheheckistan have enough problems without dumping Mom's casseroles on them, too.

Thursday 05

Dear Dumb Diary,

Because of Angeline, who thinks she is The Prettiest Girl in the World but probably is not even in the top five, I had to buy my lunch at school today. I just could not take the chance that my mom would pack a peach in my lunch again and then, while I was secretly trying to throw it in the trash, Pinsetti or Angeline would spot it and cause a big Nickname Event. Then I'd have to run away from home.

And just to prove that the entire Universe is on the side of evil, perfect Angeline, it was Meat Loaf Day in the cafeteria. Thursday is always Meat Loaf Day. The Cafeteria Monitor, Miss Bruntford, takes it personally when you don't eat something. And she gives us all kinds of grief, in particular when we don't eat the greasy cafeteria meat loaf.

Note supernatural resemblance of Bruntford to meatloaf

Miss Bruntford starts going, "What's wrong with the meat loaf?" and her giant slab of neck flubber starts waggling all over the place. She has one of those big, jiggly necks that looks like it might be soft and fluffy like the meringue on top of a lemon meringue pie.

So I had no choice but to eat some of the meat loaf, which smells a little like a wet cat, and that is Angeline's fault, too, as is everything.

Poke

One time a kid touched her Neck-FLUB AND DOCTORS DECLARED Him MEDICALLY GROSSED-OUT.

Friday 06

Dear Dumb Diary,

I don't know if I've ever mentioned Angeline before, but she's this girl at my school who is beautiful and popular and has hair the color of spun gold as if anybody likes that color.

Isabella and I were in the hallway today, and Isabella insanely tried to engage Angeline in conversation as she walked by, which was way out of line for Isabella since Angeline is like a "9" in popularity while Isabella is hovering around an unsteady "5." (And after Isabella's lip balm-dependent lips start decaying from Lip Smacker withdrawal, who knows how low that number could go?)

Anyway, Angeline just kind of looks at Isabella as if she's something peculiar and mildly gross like an inside-out nostril, and without saying a word, Angeline just keeps walking.

ISABELLA

Have you **EVER** known somebody like Angeline, Diary? Like maybe at the store where I bought you, there was some other really expensive diary that thought it was so cool that it walked around the store looking like it had a pen stuck up its binding?

Honestly, Dear Dumb Diary, if there **WAS** a diary like Angeline at the store, and you told me about it, I would go straight to the store and buy it and use its pages to pick up Stinker's you-know-whats when I take him for a walk. But also I would remind you to be happy with who you are, because you are beautiful and especially to be happy with your own hair, even though you don't have hair. But, you know, if you did and if it was real ugly.

ALSO GOOD idea

Goat EATING STUCK-UP DIARY

Isabella later told me that she thought she actually might be able to persuade Angeline to abandon ChocoMint. Isabella is a nice girl and I really like her, but if brains were bananas, let's just say that there would be a lot of skinny monkeys scraping around the inside of Isabella's skull.

Einstein's   Isabella's

DOES YOUR SKULL MONKEY LOOK AS BAD IN A BIKINI AS IT SHOULD?

PS: Nickname Update: Nobody has called me Peach Girl . . . *YET*. Angeline must be waiting for just the right time to spring it on me. It is a **KNOWN SCIENTIFIC FACT** that girls who are all pretty and Pure Goodness on the outside are Pure Evil inside.

Angeline is probably just waiting for the exact most embarrassing moment to unveil the Peach Girl nickname to the world.

true person

Saturday 07

Dear Dumb Diary,

Okay, okay. I know what I wrote yesterday about being happy with your own hair color. Maybe I was trying to be open-minded about accepting people with perfect blond hair, or maybe I was trying to be a scientist or something, but today I decided to buy one of those hair dye kits you can use at home. (You probably have never noticed, Dumb Diary, but the truth is: I have some hair issues.)

I picked the one that looked like Angeline's hair color, which they call "Glorious Heavenly Sunshine." I was not trying to copy Angeline, it just happened to be the first one I grabbed in the fourth store I looked.

I probably should have asked Isabella to help me with the hair dye but I didn't really want to get a lecture from her about self-acceptance while I pretended not to notice she was afflicted with a rapidly advancing case of what doctors call, "Lizard Lips."

I just locked myself in the bathroom and dyed alone.

A MEDICAL STUDY of LIZARD LIPS

STAGE 1

STAGE 2

STAGE 3

STAGE 4
(30 DAYS LATER)

(Which reminds me: I know why they call it "dye." Because after you see what it does, that's what you'll want to do.)

What was supposed to come out as "Glorious Heavenly Sunshine" came out the exact color of raw chicken. I could have hidden in the poultry case at the supermarket and been perfectly camouflaged.

So now I had to go back to the store and get a kit that would dye my hair back to its original color before Isabella or my mom could get on my case for not loving myself.

I pulled a clump of my old hair out of my brush so I could match it at the store, which didn't really strike me as gross until I saw how the clerk reacted when I handed it to her to help me find the right color. Luckily, they had the correct shade, and I brought it home and dyed my hair back.

By the way, you know how the name for Angeline's hair color is "Glorious Heavenly Sunshine"? The people at the dye company named the one that matches mine "Groundhog."

Sunday 08

Dear Dumb Diary,

Isabella came over much too early today (I was so glad that my hair was back the way that nature had inflicted).

She came over so early, in fact, that she actually saw my dad in his ugly plaid bathrobe that she said looks like he stole it off a homeless zombie, but I think looks *way* worse.

Anyway, Isabella just completed her Loser Scale, which identifies how much of a Loser somebody is, and therefore is a useful guide by which Loser-ness can be measured.

Isabella says that this is how the metric system started: that somebody just like her woke up one day and decided that a liter was a liter and pretty soon everybody agreed (even though nobody knows how much a liter actually is).

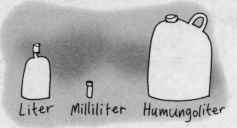

Liter   Milliliter   Humungoliter

Isabella will probably be a Professor of Popularity Science one day.

Here is Isabella's Metric System of Dorkology:

Sunday 08 (late-breaking news)

Dear Dumb Diary,

After Isabella finished making me study her Dorkology System, I talked her into going up to the store to try to choose a new lip balm flavor. (She SO did not want to do it, but I made her. This sort of Gentle Pressure is part of the grieving process when somebody loses a loved one such as ChocoMint flavoring.)

Even though Isabella made me stand there forever while she rejected about forty perfectly good lip treatments, I had to tell her that the jumbo lip gloss she finally selected and liked was actually a roll-on deodorant.

So the effort was a huge failure, but I'm sorry: Friends tell friends they're wearing antiperspirants on their mouths.

EVEN GROSSER THAN it SOUNDS

Monday 09

Dear Dumb Diary,

School was okay today. Actually, it was *better* than okay. Angeline got her long, beautiful hair tangled in one of the jillion things she has dangling from her backpack and the school nurse — who is now one of my main heroes — took a pair of scissors and snipped two feet of silky blond hair from the left side of her head, so now Angeline only looks like The Prettiest Girl in the World if you're standing on her right. (Although personally, I think she would look better if I was standing on her neck.)

Also, I got an assignment in English class to do a report on mythology. I asked my teacher Mr. Evans what "mythology" meant exactly, and he said it's about things that don't exist. I asked if that would include the hair on the left side of Angeline's head, which got a pretty good laugh from everyone except Mr. Evans and Angeline.

Mr. Evans said that I pretty much need an A on my mythology report or my grades would be with the mermaids. "You know," he said, "Below C level."

Pretty funny, huh? I hope beautiful silky, blond hair grows on his big shiny bald head so that the nurse can cut half of it off.

Tuesday 10

Dear Dumb Diary,

How weird am I?

I had to go down to the school nurse today because I think Mom may have accidentally poisoned me with some sort of mushy noodley stuff we had with dinner last night that tasted almost exactly like socks smell.

I was hoping the nurse could give me some medicine or something, but she couldn't. She just had me lie quietly on a little cot for a while. Evidently, this is how they taught her to unpoison people.

me dying

It was pretty boring, of course, just lying there trying my hardest not to be poisoned, and I started looking around. And that's when I saw it in the wastebasket: A huge clump of long, beautiful blond hair. **Angeline's** hair.

And here's the weird part: I took it. I don't know why I took it — it's not like I know how to do voodoo against her or anything.

Yet.

I just wanted it.

me escaping with clump

And in case you're worried, Dumb Diary, it turns out I wasn't poisoned after all. The nurse said I probably just had a little "dyspepsia," which I think is the medical way to say that I had a humongous, gigantic amount of gas that could choke a horse.

Wednesday 11

Dear Dumb Diary,

I tried to figure out something to do with Angeline's hair clump today. There's not quite enough to make a decent wig. I thought about planting it like a bush to see if it would grow and grow until I had actually grown another Angeline head. But then I worried it might be more beautiful than the real first head, so forget that.

I guess for now I'll just keep it like a trophy, kind of like you might keep a moose's head on the wall, except that in this case I only got a wad of the moose's hair.

On the subject of her head, Angeline was wearing a little beret on it today to cover up her butchered haircut. (*Beret* is French for stupid hat). Anyway, nobody could believe how totally goony it looked. I'm sure this will be the end for her and Hudson.

Thursday 12

Dear Dumb Diary,

Like, half the people at school were wearing berets today (including **Hudson**!!!). It's like they were all secret beret-owners, just waiting for a signal from Angeline that it was okay to start wearing their berets. I don't understand it. What if Angeline had accidentally worn her underpants on her head? I think we all know *exactly* what would have happened. Half the school would have been walking around peeking out the leg holes of their boxers.

IDIOT Buffoon half-wit

There are only two things about this that really bug me:

1) People only like Angeline because she is totally beautiful and nice and smart.

2) I don't have a beret.

It was Meat Loaf Day again today, like it is every Thursday. The Cafeteria Monitor, Miss Bruntford, made a big deal (again) about the uneaten meat loaf, but the kids who were wearing their dumb berets were all kind of unified, like the French Resistance, and they just ignored her. This made her even madder, and I noticed that she waggled her neck blubber extra furiously at Angeline, as if she knew that the berets were all Angeline's fault.

Food-Crime Update: Mom made something for dinner that was so bad, I decided to chance the lecture on Wheretheheckistan and sneak it to Stinker, my beagle. Stinker tried a bite and then, to get the taste out of his mouth, went and ate half of the grit in the cat box.

Now I am a little bit afraid of Stinker, who I think might blame me for how sick he got later, although it was totally Mom's fault and if he is planning on biting somebody's neck while they sleep, it should not be mine. (Dumb Diary, I am saying this out loud as I write so that Stinker can hear me.)

vengeful beagle

43

Friday 13

Dear Dumb Diary,

It's only about one week until my cousin gets here and Mom and Dad are on **FULL CHILD SAFETY** alert.

They've been putting special indestructible childproof latches on the cabinets where we keep cleaning products and bug killers because, evidentially, little children like to eat them.

Seems like a lot of work. If we don't want kids to eat those things, wouldn't it be simpler to just make them broccoli flavored?

Saturday 14

Dear Dumb Diary,

I figured that I had better do something to prepare for the mythology thing in Mr. Evans's class.

I went online and read about Medusa, who had poisonous snakes growing out of her head, and who would have been totally jealous of a girl with real hair even if it was the color of a groundhog.

I have one piece of advice for people with poisonous vipers for hair: Ponytails. Bangs. Something.

BEFORE MAKEOVER

WORN UP IN PROM STYLE

BRAIDS

GLAMOROUS WAVE

I also read about Icarus who made wings out of wax and then flew too close to the sun and they melted. The moral is this: If Icarus had been meant to fly, he would have been born a flight attendant like my cousin Terrence.

Did you know, Dumb Diary, that mythology can include things like trolls and giants and talking fish since it wasn't just the Greeks and Romans that had mythology? Old Dead Guys everywhere had mythology, which I think is very, very interesting to somebody somewhere, maybe.

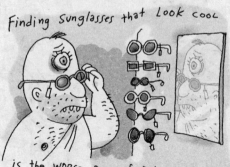

Finding sunglasses that look cool is the WORST PART of BEING A CYCLOPS

Saturday 14 (late-breaking news)

Dear Dumb Diary,

Isabella and I were out walking this afternoon and we accidentally walked about a half mile out of our way and *accidentally* found ourselves way over by Derby Street, which was a peculiar coincidence because that is sort of near where Hudson Rivers lives exactly.

Isabella said that walking past his house like this was a form of stalking, but I told her that it wasn't because stalkers are crazy, and we were sane enough to wear disguises.

 flawless disguise

The disguises turned out to be a pretty good idea because as we walked past, Hudson happened to look out the window, which freaked out Isabella who ran — but not before she pushed me down on the lawn.

I caught up to her six blocks later. She apologized, explaining that she only pushed me down before running because of what was probably just an instinct, like if a bear was chasing us.

Since it was only that, I forgave her.

Sunday 15

Dear Dumb Diary,

I finally found a beret at the mall. It cost me thirty bucks, which wiped me out, and I don't even like it, but a fad is a fad, and frankly, I'm not sure if I'm cool enough to ignore a fad. It's a very difficult thing to judge.

I heard about a girl who went to a different school and tried to ignore some huge fad, like cargo pants or something. The next thing you know her family forced her to marry her own first cousin once-removed and she went insane. Although, as I write this, I'm not sure if that has anything to do with cargo pants, and I don't even think the government lets people marry their first cousins whether they are once-removed or not. It's all probably a lie except the cargo pants and insane parts.

AAAAARAA AA

me insane

Anyway, I'm tired and it's time for bed. I'm going to try to force myself to dream that a huge toad gobbles up Angeline and then the toad is eaten by a giant hog and then the hog is made into this awful toad-flavored ham that is served at Angeline's sixteenth birthday party and everybody gets sick including Angeline who is somehow magically alive again to eat her own ghastly toad-hog-ham self.

I don't always remember my dreams but I'll know if I dream this one because I'll wake up laughing so hard my stomach will hurt.

isn't imagination a lovely thing?

Monday 16

Dear Dumb Diary,

The beret fad is over. As I threw my *thirty-dollar* beret in the trash, I wondered how could it be over so fast. Do you wonder, too, Dumb Diary? Well, stay tuned . . .

Today in science, Mr. Tweeds gave us an out-loud pop quiz where he asked everybody one question. This was the question he gave me:

"How could you determine which way north is using only a needle?"

Here is what I answered: "Find a smart person and threaten to stick it in him if he won't tell you which way north is."

Which I guess I knew was wrong, but didn't realize it was wrong enough to get you sent to the principal's office.

And by the way, Diary, here's an easy way to remember if you spell it princi**ple** or princi**pal**. (Maybe you've heard it before, Diary?) Just remember that *pal*eontology is the study of fossils that are about a *jillion* years old.

PALeontology   princi PAL

Oh. And by the way: I have solved *The Mystery of the Sudden Demise of the Beret Fad*. On my way to the principal's office I saw that all of the secretary women in the school office were wearing berets.

Thanks a lot, ladies. Maybe next time I'll take a chance on marrying cousin Terrence.

Now get this, **Dumb Diary:** While I was in his office, the principal pulled out the folder containing my permanent record to make a note of this latest smartmouthery. (As you know, your permanent record follows you through school and is not destroyed until you are married or dead or something.) But when he pulled out my folder, I noticed, just a couple folders away from mine . . . ANGELINE'S PERMANENT RECORD.

I WAS MILDLY INTERESTED

Instantly, I knew I had a goal in life: To possess and share the horrible contents of this folder with the world, and to reveal to mankind the boyfriend/scent thief that Angeline really is.

Oops. I got so excited on that last part that I dropped my diary on Stinker's head, who was asleep. And I think he might be swearing in dog language right now.

Tuesday 17

Dear Dumb Diary,

I tried to think about doing something on my mythology report today, since it's getting close to the deadline, and it's probably time to actually make some progress regarding starting to worry about it. I want to work on it, really and truly I do, but I think I may have caught a little case of **OCD** about Angeline's permanent record.

evil
SPIRiT OF
ANGELiNE'S
FOLDER ➘

➘ me
innocently
trying to do
my homework

OCD, in case you've never heard of it, Dumb Diary, stands for Obsessive-Compulsive Disorder, and it's this condition where you become obsessive and compulsive about things. It makes you think about something so much that you do things like wash your hands a hundred times a day, or open your locker over and over to make sure you haven't forgotten anything for your next class, or keep saying over and over to yourself "I must have Angeline's permanent record."

Anyway, since it's psychological, and not from germs, I'm pretty sure you can catch it from watching a talk show about it, which is how I think I may have caught it. Obviously, Mom will be calling me in sick tomorrow morning.

DISEASES YOU CAN CATCH FROM WATCHING T.V.

THINKING A MANIAC IS HIDING IN YOUR CLOSET

TALKING WITH DUMB ACCENT

OCD

KNOWLEDGE THAT THERE ARE A JILLION BRANDS OF CAT LITTER

WORRYING THAT THE MARK ON YOUR ARM IS A LITTLE BIT OF PLAGUE

Oh. And one other thing: Angeline's bald hair patch is almost totally invisible now. She has employed some sort of secret military combing technology to camouflage the patch she had been covering with the beret. It is also possible that she simply regenerated the lost hair, regrowing it the way a lizard regrows a lost tail or a slug regrows — I don't know — a big snotty lump or something that somebody cuts off him.

ANGELINE'S FREAKISH HEAD

BEFORE

AFTER

SINISTER MILITARY SECRET
OR
EVIDENCE OF SUBHUMAN PARENTS?
you decide!

Wednesday 18

Dear Dumb Diary,

Mom would not call me in sick from school today. But it's okay, because I have miraculously recovered from my OCD and actually do not even think about or care about Angeline anymore. Let me prove it. Below, I will write the names of people that I just don't care about at all.

George Washington, Ringo Starr, Christina Aguilera, Zeus, Angeline, Dan Rather, Caesar Riley, Angeline, Paul Bunyan, Cleopatra, Nefertiti, Maria Barbo, Angeline, Koko the Signing Gorilla, The Yellow Teletubby, Angeline, Angeline, Angeline, Angeline, ANGELINE

Thursday 19

Dear Dumb Diary,

Okay, okay. Maybe Angeline does still bug me a little. I just *had* to have Angeline's permanent record, and the only way to do it was to get sent to the principal's office again.

So at lunch today, Miss Bruntford, the neck-waggling cafeteria monitor, lost her mind and said that nobody could leave the cafeteria until they had finished the meat loaf. She was staring at us and we were staring at her and you could have cut the tension with a knife, which is something you can't do with the meat loaf.

SCHOOL IS AN ENDLESS BATTLE
Between the forces of GOOD AND THE
FAT-NECKED FORCES OF EVIL

Suddenly, a big honkin' slab of the shiny slippery meat loaf came flying through the air and smacked Miss Bruntford right in the neck blubber.

She started screaming and sputtering and demanding to know who did it. It seemed like a golden opportunity, so I said that I was the one who had thrown it. Easy ticket to the principal's office, right?

SPLOT

Boxer SHORTS?

I suspect so.

But get this: As they're hustling me out of the cafeteria like I'm a perp on that *COPS* show, I'm looking down at everybody's trays. I see meat loaf after meat loaf after meat loaf. And then I see one tray without meat loaf. I look up, and there's Angeline, wiping gravy off her hand with a napkin.

ANGELINE!!! She was the one that threw the meat loaf, and I had taken the fall for it.

The
GRAVY
OF
GUILT

Of course, I got a big lecture from the principal and he might have even mentioned Wheretheheckistan. Plus, he banned me from eating school lunches for two weeks. (I got the feeling that he thought that was a much worse punishment than it actually was.)

And, to make things worse, of course I did not get Angeline's permanent record. (I mean, what did I think I was going to do? Knock the principal out with a karate kick and just grab the folder out of the file cabinet???) It turns out this was a pretty lousy idea. I'm never going to try something that dumb again.

Even if you are justified like I am, kicking a PRINCIPAL'S HEAD OFF is STILL NOT ENTIRELY Right.

Friday 20

Dear Dumb Diary,

I tried something that dumb again. Between classes, I saw the principal talking to Miss Anderson who is a teacher and therefore old, but is beautiful enough to be a waitress, and all the men teachers talk to her for a long time. I ran all the way to the office and walked right in and asked to talk to the principal. He wasn't there, so one of the secretaries told me to come back later, but I told her I had a private matter to discuss with him, and could I leave him a note? Then I told her that with that beret on, I thought for a second she was one of the school cheerleaders.

She ACTUALLY Believed it.

Of course, she let me right in and all I had to do was just walk over to the cabinet and snatch Angeline's permanent record. I know what you're thinking, Dumb Diary: You are thinking that I am the Smartest Chick in the World. And you're right. I *am* the Smartest Chick in the World.

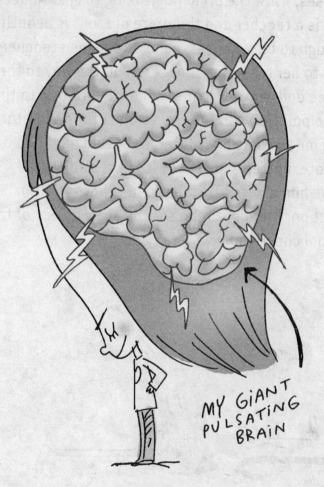

MY GIANT PULSATING BRAIN

And later on, the Smartest Chick in the World forgot Angeline's file at school. On a *Friday*. So now I'll have **OCD** about it all weekend.

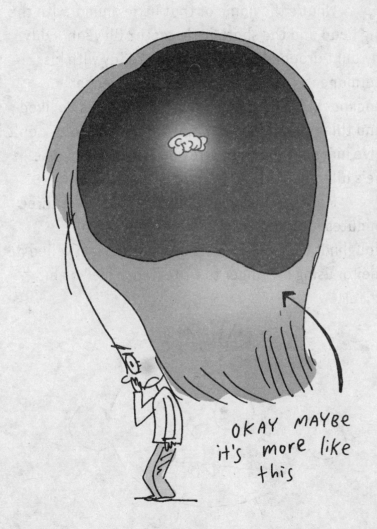

OKAY MAYBe it's more like this

Saturday 21

Dear Dumb Diary,

What's the name of that little animal with the big head and the sharp little teeth? Oh yeah: Eddy. My aunt dropped off Cousin Eddy today with his permanently sticky face and Robot Avenger backpack. She had a big long list of things he liked and things he didn't, but most of all, she said, don't give him anything with strawberries in it because he's allergic.

Mom keeps washing his face, but, like, three minutes later he's sticky again. He's like a doughnut that secretes its own glaze. Mom yelled at me for using my finger to write "wash me" on his cheek.

Sunday 22

Dear Dumb Diary,

    Angeline uses such a wonderful and important shampoo that the small wad of hair I have has actually made our whole house smell better. It also has a powerful effect on Eddy, who seems to have an unnatural love for it, and a mutant ability to sniff it out of its hiding places.

    My Scientific Theory is that since Eddy will grow up into a Guy one day, he is already instinctively and unnaturally in love with Angeline. The hair has no effect on my dad, and Isabella says that is because he is my dad and stopped being a Guy when he met my mom.

    The fragrance also seems to have an effect on Stinker, who sneezes and sneezes whenever I grind the hair wad in his face. I wonder if that annoys him?

SNARL
GRRR
GRR

ZOMBIE-
LIKE
DEVOTION
TO
HAIR WAD

Monday 23

Dear Dumb Diary,

There's good news and there's bad news. The good news is Mom says that my aunt is picking up Eddy on Thursday, which is a relief because I'm getting tired of trying to hide Angeline's hair wad from him. There's more good news. I remembered to bring Angeline's permanent record home. But I set it down one second and turned my back and when I reached for it again it was gone. I know it was either Stinker or Eddy who took it, but no amount of yelling or depriving of toys or dog bones has had any effect. And Eddy really likes those bones.

WHICH ONE IS GUILTY?

The mangy flea-Bitten Animal or the dog?

Tuesday 24

Dear Dumb Diary,

It is making me mental that Angeline's permanent record is in this house and I cannot find it. I even looked in Stinker's doghouse, which meant I had to throw out all the sticks and trash he had been keeping in there. Since then, Stinker has been staring at me for hours with his black, black, dog eyes and I think he may be planning something against me.

Maybe I should buy a dozen big mean cats to have around the house in case some mean little dog shows up to try to do something mean to me. (Dumb Diary, I read that last sentence out loud so that Stinker could hear it, but it did not seem to have any effect on him. If I turn up missing in the morning, I just hope the police dust for fingerprints, or foot prints, or whatever you call the prints left by those paw-nubs on the bottom of a guilty beagle's foot. Hint, hint.)

BIG MEAN CAT
ARE You Getting all this, Stinker?

Wednesday 25

Dear Dumb Diary,

I'm angry on the outside . . .

. . . but I'm far angrier on the inside.

I finally finished my mythology report. In spite of distractions, like cousin Eddy clawing at the door to get in, and the frustrating knowledge that there could be something so joyfully horrendous in Angeline's folder that it could be used to reduce her to a tiny quivering lump of sobbing goo, and I do not know where the folder is.

Happily, Mom told me that Eddy won't be here much longer — my aunt is meeting us at school tomorrow morning to pick him up.

I wonder if I'll miss having him around the house? I didn't miss Stinker's Frantic Itchy Butt Disease when that cleared up, so I think I'll be okay when Eddy is gone.

THE WORLD OF THE BEAGLE
DOES IT REVOLVE AROUND HIS BUTT?

Itches a little

Itches medium

Total freak-out knock-a-table-over itchiness

Asleep but it still itches

Thursday 26

Dear Dumb Diary,

Stinker ate my mythology report.

I guess at least now I know what he's been planning. He was waiting for me to finish it. Here's how I know he was doing it to get back at me: He only ate the words. He left the paper margins in his bowl like pizza crusts.

I had to pack my own lunch this morning, on account of being banned from buying lunch at school. There was only a spoonful of strawberry jam for my sandwich and just to make things worse, Stinker must have licked it off my bread while I went to the fridge to look for a juice box. I figured he did it to get the taste of mythology out his mouth — which probably tastes awful — so I didn't even get that mad at him. My mom finished packing my lunch and stuck it in my backpack.

Mythology might taste worse than Mom's cooking

So there I was, Dumb Diary. Mom was dropping me off at school, and I knew I was headed for an "F" from Mr. Evans. I mean, you just can't actually *say* the dog ate your homework. I have to give that mean little beagle credit: Stinker played that one beautifully.

While I was headed into school, my aunt met my mom outside, and they were getting ready to transfer Eddy from one minivan to another when he escaped, I guess.

And the way I know that is because while I was walking the Walk of the Condemned toward Mr. Evans's class, a small, dirty savage went whipping past me in the halls with his little Robot Avenger backpack followed by my screaming aunt. I was just about to grab Eddy for her when I noticed Hudson walking past, and I had to quickly decide if I was going to help a family member or try to look cool for a guy that probably hardly knows I'm alive.

"Hi, Hudson," I said as Eddy scrambled out of sight around the corner followed by my aunt who I think was starting to cry.

I walked into Mr. Evans's class, knowing full well that I would be going first. Mr. Evans called on me to stand up in front of the class and give my presentation.

I had just started to say "Mr. Evans, I don't have my —" when Eddy ran into the class. His face was swollen and his tongue was so thick I couldn't understand whatever he was jabbering. I suddenly knew that Stinker had not licked my bread this morning — Eddy had. I guess he really *is* allergic to strawberries. Eddy was so puffy he looked like a picture of himself somebody had drawn on a balloon.

Before   After

Eddy saw my backpack at the same time I saw him use his supernatural hair-wad-locating-ability against me, and we both lunged for it. But the little demon-child was faster, and he managed to get his big round head inside the backpack before I could stop him. When I finally pulled his head out, he had Angeline's hair clump stuck like a beard to his always-sticky face. With his dirty clothes and beard and weird swollen-faced jabbering, he didn't seem human.

The fact that I was holding Eddie around his neck as he kicked and growled and clawed at the air did not do much to create the impression that he was a human being, either.

Mr. Evans jumped to his feet and turned red and started bulging his forehead vein at us and was all "Do you know this . . . child, Jamie?" That's when I realized that the next thing out of my mouth was going to get me failed, and also nicknamed throughout the school as the Girl with the Crazy Cousin, or something worse: Mike Pinsetti was quickly jotting down a few nickname ideas on a sheet of paper. You could tell he was trying out a few things. I thought about pitching Eddy out the second-story window.

Then, it happened. Eddy had knocked my lunch bag out of my backpack, and what comes rolling out and stops right in front of me? A **PEACH**. My mom had packed a *peach*.

Angeline stood up. This was it. This was her big opportunity. She had waited for just the right moment, and this was obviously **IT**.

Angeline walked to the front of the class, and stood next to me. She smiled her perfect Angeline smile and said, "Mr. Evans, Jamie and I did our report together. We did it on trolls. And this," she said, pointing to Eddy, "is our visual aid."

She didn't call me Peach Girl. She didn't do anything bad. Angeline was **ACTUALLY HELPING ME**. Mr. Evans and the whole class — even Hudson — suddenly looked like they were getting this giant backrub from Angeline's voice, which is the most beautiful mortal voice ever heard, but so what?

people melted into puddle of sick love for ANGELINE

My butt was on the line here. So, I went with it. The two of us started making it up as we went along and every time Eddy would snarl or growl the whole class would laugh, and I think Eddy even started to like it. I quickly realized this was the best report I had ever given, and I was actually enjoying giving it. Just as we finished, my aunt showed up at the door and took Eddy away, and we got an A on the report and even a round of applause. (Isabella had to do her best not to smile. Her lips are so dry now that even a slight smile will split them open like a pair of burnt hot dogs.)

As I went back to my desk, I asked myself:
Why would Angeline help me out? Could
it have been because I took the fall for her meat
loaf crime? Were we supposed to be friends now?
The thought of it just made me totally ill. I looked
SO sick, in fact, that Mr. Evans told me to get my
stuff and go down to the school nurse.

How could
Evans tell
that I
felt
sick?

When I went for my bag, I saw Eddy's Robot Avenger backpack on the floor next to it, and peeking out of just one little corner, I saw Angeline's permanent record. I scooped it up and headed for the nurse's office.

How I tried to Look

How I probably Looked

The nurse did what she always does. It doesn't matter if you have a heart attack, a leg eaten off by bear, or an ax stuck in your face, it's always the same thing: **Lie Down on the Cot and Rest.**

ILLNESSES OUR NURSE TRIES TO CURE WITH THE COT

HEADACHE

SWALLOWED BY PYTHON

RACCOON MISHAP

NOTHING LEFT BUT SKELETON

While I was lying there, I looked at the cover of Angeline's permanent record. Before I opened it, I amused myself with what might be inside: Maybe counterfeiting, kidnapping, fixing the outcome of school football games by means of insincere eyelash-batting at quarterbacks.

Or maybe she had been brought up on charges of spending her whole life as somebody who people can't help but like even though deep down they really and truly want to hate her.

All that was left to do was open it, and read it, and then share its terrible contents with the World.

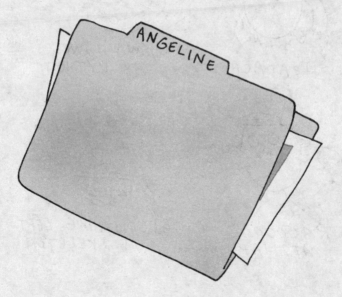

Friday 27

Dear Dumb Diary,

Angeline sat down across from Isabella and me at lunch today. I was eating a ham-and-cheese sandwich that I had packed for lunch but we were all out of cheese, and I had felt guilty about how I had treated Stinker so I had given him the last slice of ham as a truce. I guess you would call it a mustard sandwich if I had remembered to put mustard on it.

Who Doesn't enjoy a nice nothing Sandwich?

(By the way, Stinker and I are pals again. I guess he figured that eating my homework had made us even for the last couple of weeks. Thinking back, I suppose that **WAS** fair.)

Okay, back to Angeline (remember Angeline?). Incredibly, between bites of bread, I actually said this to Angeline: "Thanks for saving my life on the report yesterday." I didn't actually intend to be polite. I've been brainwashed by my parents to be polite against my will sometimes.

Then she smiled at me. And it wasn't totally an Aren't-I-Great-with-My-Perfect-Teeth-and-Gums-Smile. It was a regular smile. And she said, "We should do something sometime. A movie or something. Maybe you can teach me how to do that thing you do with your hair," she said, pointing at my head. "I can never get my hair to do anything cool."

CONFUSINGLY NON-EVIL

And the very next thing I knew, Dumb Diary, Miss Bruntford, the Cafeteria Monitor had me in a Heimlich position and was trying to disgorge a bread chunk that I had accidentally inhaled when Angeline had complimented my hair. After a couple squeezes, up it came, and I saw Mike Pinsetti standing there, grinning. It was obvious that he had crafted some excellent nickname for me that he was about to unveil, and everybody was waiting to hear what it was going to be, when Angeline grabbed him by the collar and said, "Just don't, **PIN-HEADY**."

SQUISH

CHOKING CAN KILL YOU.

HUMILIATION CAN ALMOST MAKE YOU WISH IT HAD.

OINK

SPLAT

PIN-HEADY. It was a masterpiece of nicknaming. It rhymed with his real name, it was insulting, and everybody in the cafeteria was standing there to hear it used for the first time. Even though he was utterly shattered, you could see a reluctant respect on Mike's face.

Other things you could see on his face...

CONSTELLATIONS OF PIMPLES

ONE UNBROKEN EYEBROW

SAUCE? INFECTION? NOBODY KNOWS

AN EXCELLENT PLACE FOR A HORSE TO KICK

A NEVER-CLOSED MOUTH

Angeline, who no one even knew had any cruelty within her at all, had shown the meanness that Isabella and I had always known was there.

I sure hope people DON'T WORSHIP ME TOO MUCH FOR REVEALING THE TRUTH

Sure, she had only been cruel to Pin-heady (look how I am already forgetting his real name) and, yes, she kind of saved my neck again by not letting him get off a nickname for me, but c'mon, at least the world now knew that she's not this total perfect angel.

I know what you're thinking, Dumb Diary: Use the old one-two punch. I have her permanent record to share with the World. I can fix her once and for all.

Except that I *don't* have it anymore. Yesterday I had decided not to read Angeline's permanent record. I just slipped out of the nurse's office and into the principal's office and put it back in the file cabinet.

Besides, I thought, this is Angeline, how bad could it have **REALLY** been?

Isabella's lips cleared up a couple hours after lunch. It was like a miracle. They turned from what looked like sad little splintered slivers of beef jerky into what looks like full, ripe luscious crescents of papaya.

It was the meat loaf. The mysterious meat it's made from had some sort of incredible healing power on Isabella's lips. And it's her new signature flavor. She stuffed a wad of it into an old lip-balm tube. I know. It's awful. But it smells better than ChocoMint.

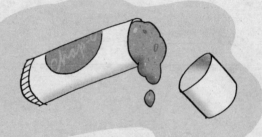

But that was only the second weirdest thing that the Universe did today.

Later on, after school, Angeline walked right up to me.

"I forgot to say thanks," she said.

"For what?" I said.

"For taking the blame for my meat loafing of the monitor."

And then, when she said that, IT
happened. I felt the entire Universe groan and
creak and shift slightly, and the next thing I knew,
her terrible Angeline powers were starting to work
on me. I felt as though I might be starting to LIKE
ANGELINE AGAINST MY WILL.

I told Angeline it was no big deal. I had always wanted to do that myself.

"No, no. It *was* a big deal," she said. "You have no idea how much trouble I would have gotten in. If you could see what my permanent record looks like, you'd know. One more incident, and I'd be out of here and you'd have Hudson all to yourself, and I am **NOT** going to let that happen." Then she smiled and walked away.

I stood there for a while, Dumb Diary, sort of like a black-eyed beagle who has just seen all of his most precious sticks and trash thrown out by someone who has mistaken him for someone he is not. I was frozen in my spot by feelings of affection and hatred all glopped together like one of Mom's inedible Food-Crimes.

Maybe people are like meat loaf: Strong medicine, but also deadly poison.

I wondered, as Mike Pinsetti walked by me without making eye contact, if I could find the wisdom that Stinker had found and could exact the precise amount of justice called for here, which was to simply eat Angeline's homework sometime, and then call it even.

WELL, IT'S STILL PROBABLY BETTER THAN MOM'S COOKING.

Thanks for listening, Dumb Diary.

Jamie Kelly

THIS DIARY PROPERTY
OF
Jamie Kelly

SCHOOL: MACKEREL MIDDLE School

Locker: 101

Best friend: Isabella

Pet: Stinker (beagle)

Occupation: FASHion expert and makeover guru

UNLESS you are me,

I command you to stop reading now.

if you are me,
sorry, it's cool

Dear Whoever Is Reading My Dumb Diary,

Are you sure you're supposed to be reading somebody else's diary? Have you done this before? If I did not give YOU permission, YOU had better stop right now.

If you are my parents, then YES, I know that I am not allowed to call people idiots and fools and goons and half-wits and gerds and all that, but this is a diary, and I didn't actually "call" them anything. I *wrote* it. And if you punish me for it, then I will know that you read my diary, which I am *not* giving you permission to do.

Now, by the power vested in me, I do promise that everything in this diary is true, or at least as true as I think it needs to be.

Signed,

Jamie Kelly

PS: If this is you, Angeline, reading this, then you are officially busted. I happen to have this entire room under hidden video surveillance. And, in just a moment, little doors will slide open and flesh-eating rats will stream into the room. And, like tiny venomous cowboys, scorpions will be riding the rats. So it's curtains for you, Angeline! Mwah-hah-hah-hah!

SNIP

I love Animals

PSS: If this is you, Margaret or Sally, then HA-HA — you are also caught in my surveillance sting.

PSSS: If this is you, Isabella, don't you ever get tired of reading my diary? I mean, I've caught you doing it, like, nine or ten times, so just STOP IT. Seriously. Maybe you should see somebody about this.

Dear Jamie-
I am <u>so</u> sure. I do <u>NOT</u> read your diary. So get over yourself.

-Isabella

PS- I totally agree with the stuff you said about your mom.

Sunday 01

Dear Dumb Diary,

   Mom and I got into a "discussion" about fashion after dinner tonight. Of course, she really has no idea what the trends are at my school. I told her that I think she can't possibly know how important trends can be, and she said that clothes were just as important when she was in middle school. Then I said that I understood how she probably always tried her best to make a good impression on Fred and Wilma and Barney and the whole gang down at the tar pit, but times had changed.

a typical mother-daughter discussion

And that's just part of the reason I'm here in my room way ahead of schedule for the evening. Here's the exchange that followed my Mom-Is-Old-As-Cavemen joke:

"Just how do you think that makes me feel?" Mom asked.

"Stupid?" I guessed.

MOST DANGEROUS THINGS ON EARTH

BEAR THAT CAN BURP UP HAND GRENADES

GIANT SHARK WITH LITTLE SHARKS FOR TEETH

MY MOM WHEN YOU'RE TRYING TO MAKE HER ANGRY

Turns out that Mom had a different answer in mind, and I'll have a little time to figure out what it was since I'm here in my bedroom about five hours earlier than usual.

I also think that Dad sitting there trying **not** to laugh might have made things worse.

You can always tell when Dad is trying not to laugh

Sometimes diaries can be so much easier to talk to than moms. I can't picture Mom letting me write on her face, and I imagine sliding a bookmark in somewhere would result in a major wrestling match.

Monday 02

Dear Dumb Diary,

Angeline is back to her old tricks, Dumb Diary.

Yeah, sure, for a long time, everything was fine between us. (Nearly four whole days — except two of those were over the weekend, during which I did not see her.) But then today, in science class, while I was talking to Hudson Rivers (eighth cutest guy in my grade), she performed an act of **UTTER BEAUTY** and distracted him.

Actually, I hadn't started to talk to him yet, but I was going to, and she should have known that when she whipped out her **GORGEOUSNESS** and waved it all over the place.

Isn't it time we stopped the beautiful people?

It's true. I may not be fully qualified to talk to Hudson Rivers. Maybe he *is* just slightly too cute for me. (I'm right on the edge of adorable.) But if I'm really, really lucky and keep my fingers crossed, he could become mildly disfigured. Then we'd be on the same level, and I want to make sure I'm ready should that blessed maiming occur.

SQUOOSH

A Beautiful thought
You are just one Rampaging Elephant away from marrying the Handsomest Boy in the school

And besides, Angeline is in that Mega-Popular category where she can probably go and work her wicked charms against boys like Chip, who is the number one cutest boy in the school.

So why does she always have to perform acts of **Beauty** around Hudson?

(Chip, like Madonna and Cher and Moses, only goes by his first name. I'm not sure anybody knows what his last name is.)

Other one-Namers

PINK

TARZAN

BEEPY

THE SCIENCE of BOY-OLOGY
Local Specimens

CHIP
CUTENESS RANKING: **1**

NON-MEAN AND HANDSOME ENOUGH TO BE IN A SHAVING CREAM COMMERCIAL

HUDSON RIVERS
CUTENESS RANKING: **8**

EASILY TRICKED INTO THINKING ANGELINE IS PRETTY. OTHERWISE EXCELLENT

ROSCO
(CHIP'S) DOG
CUTENESS RANKING: **19**

STRICTLY SPEAKING NOT A BOY, BUT CUTER AND WAY MORE POPULAR THAN MOST TRUE BOYS

MIKE PINSETTI
CUTENESS RANKING: **ALMOST LAST**

MEAN AND MOUTHY. IF YOU MEET HIM TELL HIM ALL ABOUT SOAP.

THAT ONE KID
CUTENESS RANKING: **LAST**

DOES HE EVEN HAVE A NAME? WHO KNOWS. HE DOESN'T SEEM TO NEED ONE

Tuesday 03

Dear Dumb Diary,

Isabella came by after school to root through my magazines for those little paper perfume samples. She's got a top secret fragrance project she's working on. It's connected to her ongoing obsession with **Popularity,** I'm sure of it. Isabella is kind of an expert on Popularity, or so she says. (I know: Isabella belongs in a cage. But she is my best friend, **So One Does What One Must.**)

I looked everywhere before I finally found my magazines. Get this: they were in my parents' room. Hmmm! Looked like Mom had been flipping through them. I wonder if she's planning to do some sort of makeover on herself.

AN EXCELLENT MOM MAKEOVER

I heard about this girl whose mom had a makeover done on herself, and it was so good that afterward the mom looked younger and hotter than the daughter, which made her feel so guilty that she decided to have the makeover unmade. But when the cosmetologists tried to undo what had been done, they said that her body had absorbed the makeover, and now she was permanently afflicted with **Hotness.**

So her daughter came down with a form of **Embarrassment** that has to be treated by doctors.

Honestly, I'm not terribly worried about Mom having a makeover. She can hardly makeover a bed.

mom makes a bed

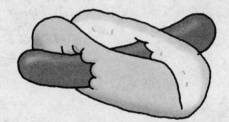

mom makes a hot dog

Wednesday 04

Dear Dumb Diary,

Here are what some people think are the worst things about my school:

 When the Bus Drivers dress up for Halloween

 The unmistakable tangy flavor of horse organs in the cafeteria meatloaf.

When the teachers try talking cool

But they're wrong...

The worst thing about school is my science class. I like the *idea* of science. I mean, it comforts me to know that Angeline's guts are no more glorious or appealing than the stuff you'd scoop out of a porcupine.

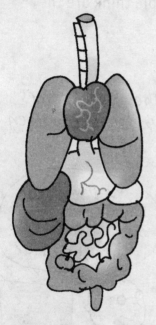

porcupine
guts

pretty girl
guts

you decide

But it's the whole chemistry part of it that I hate, like "this-kind-of-stuff-can-burn-through-this-junk," and "when-you-mix-this-with-that-then-whatever-will-explode." Science just doesn't seem to have much to do with what I'm trying to accomplish in my life right now, which is mainly the avoidance of science.

Are they even sure they want me in science class?

BOOM

At least Hudson Rivers is in my class. Isabella and I sometimes exchange scientific observations on Hudson.

Specimen chews gum at a rate of 32 chomps per minute

Specimen's right eye is 8% cuter than left eye

Specimen becomes mildly creeped out when it notices somebody counting its gum chews

Thursday 05

Dear Dumb Diary,

    Tonight at dinner I realized that I am, once again, the youngest person in my family. My beagle, Stinker, was once younger than me, but by employing the totally unfair dog trick of aging seven years in just twelve months, Stinker went from peeing on the carpet to being old enough to drive in just a couple years. He is the only member of my family who has ever accomplished such an amazing feat, except I think I have an uncle who might have done it, too.

    It is for this reason that I decided not to give Stinker my table scraps after dinner this evening. (Not because my uncle peed, but because Stinker made me the baby of the family *again*.)

Beagle actually trying to age 7 times faster than me.

This really made Stinker mad. Tonight, dinner was Chinese food — almost a beagle's favorite meal. (I wonder what they call Chinese food in China. They probably just say, "Here. Here's some of that food we always have.")

Friday 06

Dear Dumb Diary,

The vengeful beagle strikes again. To get back at me for not giving him my table scraps, Stinker ate a huge hole out of the backside of my only clean pair of jeans. (The second-best pair in the collection.) I know he would say he had to do it because he was so hungry from not having his normal gut-full of table scraps, but I know that he did it out of revenge.

How can I be so sure Stinker made the hole? It was in the most embarrassing place possible and it was **PERFECTLY** round. It looked like a tailor had chewed it.

Tailors are clothing experts and could probably bite a hole of any shape

So, I had to go with a pair of khaki pants that really had no business being out on a Friday. They're a Sunday pair of khakis. Sure, they started as a Friday pair of pants, but as cooler pants were purchased, the khakis were demoted.

I paired them with a shirt that was a *serious* Friday shirt, hoping to boost the khakis' confidence and give them the feeling that maybe they were somehow becoming more fashionable. It totally worked, of course, as pants are really stupid. You would think that a pair of khakis would notice that, currently, the most popular pants at my school are jeans, faded to just the right shade of blue.

PHASES IN THE LIFE of PANTS

PHASE 1
Brand new and in style. Happiest time in a pant's life. Wear at any time.

PHASE 2
Slightly out of style or with taco stain. Wear on Sundays only.

PHASE 3
Hole bitten out of fanny by dog or tailor. Wear only as part of Hobo costume.

Of course, I don't *have* any jeans that are the perfect shade of blue. If I awoke one morning to discover that I had a pair that **WAS** the right shade of blue, I would just assume that they weren't my pants, it wasn't my house, and it wasn't me who had just woken up.

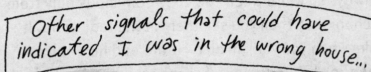
Other signals that could have indicated I was in the wrong house...

Dad encourages massive make-up abuse

Dog is not mean and spends several minutes a day not licking itself

Mom prepares a nonstinking casserole which family voluntarily eats

Saturday 07

Dear Dumb Diary,

The most incredible thing happened today. Isabella and I saw Angeline, but not at school. It's always so weird when you know somebody only from school, but then you see them in the real world. It's like when you walk in on a clown, and he's only wearing his underpants. (Long story: Bad birthday party experience. Don't like clowns anymore.)

Anyway, Angeline was in the park, and she was playing with these two little kids who Isabella and I figured were her little sisters. But the little sisters did not have Angeline's great looks (**Nobody cares anyway, Angeline!**), thereby verifying what we have always just suspected about Angeline: **SHE'S BEEN PLASTIC-SURGEONED.** Probably nothing on her is an original part.

It would cost a fortune to do that much plastic surgery on somebody who started out as ugly as we hope Angeline did, so we figure that Angeline's dad is some big doctor.

On top of everything else, she's probably RICH.

ANALYSIS of THE Surgery they probably did on ANGELINE

HORN REMOVAL $1500

HAIR DYED AND MADE PERMANENTLY GOOD SMELLING $1800

CONTACT LENSES $800

NOSE JOB $4200

WING TRIM $2000

FANGECTOMY $1800

TAIL CUT OFF

EXTREME MANICURE $47

KNEES DE-KNOBBED

FEET PROBABLY LEFT THE SAME

Just when I thought I knew everything there was about Angeline that bugged me, it turns out she's also loaded.

Angeline taking a BATH IN PURE MONEY

Jewel encrusted soap

Hot and cold running diamonds

Rug of extraordinary fluffiness

Sunday 08

Dear Dumb Diary,

It's Sunday. Also known as **Homework Day**. Every weekend I tell myself that I'm going to finish my homework when I get home on Friday afternoon, and then I tell myself I'm going to do it Saturday morning, and then I tell myself I'll do it Saturday night, and then I tell myself to get off my back, and why am I always nagging myself, and then I call myself a name and have to apologize to myself.

And then I have to do all my homework on Sunday.

Tomorrow is school and I can't risk another wardrobe-munching by Stinker, so I gave him table scraps from dinner.

How Beagles enjoy their scraps

Sniff suspiciously for eleven minutes

SNIFF SNURF SNURF SNIFF

cautiously pick up with front teeth

PINCE

Hork it down in one gulp and choke to death a little

GWARF ACK GAG GULP

Monday 09

Dear Dumb Diary,

Okay. Who wants to buy a beagle cheap? Remember the other night we had Chinese food? Stinker didn't get any scraps and that's why he ate my pants.

Last night I gave him scraps, but Mom had cooked some sort of **Goo Casserole** and it had somehow slipped my mind that few living things except bacteria enjoy my mom's cooking. (Mom is a good mom and everything, but she's not very good at traditional mom things, like cooking and cleaning and washing clothes.) So *guess* what Stinker did?

pure love
and joy

utter
disgust

It looks like Stinker quietly crept through the house, carefully sorted through the laundry Mom had just done, found the absolute **best**-looking pair of jeans I own, and ate an even bigger hole. Through the front this time!

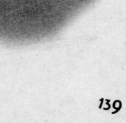

pure evil

Does anybody **know** why dogs do the things they do? I think they might do some of them (like *you-know-what*) just to see if they can get their picture in the newspaper for being the **GROSSEST DOG ON EARTH.** But why Stinker is gnawing through my pants is anybody's guess.

The Daily News

DOG DOES GROSSEST THING ANYBODY EVER HEARD OF

"SO DID WE" CLAIM OTHER LOCAL DOGS

The couch it happened behind

I could propose the question in science class, except it would draw attention to my pants and I had to wear khakis again today.

Our science class works like this: Everybody has a lab partner. A lab partner is a person that you do all the experiments with while you both wish the other one was Sally Winthorpe, who is this really smart girl who probably has a brain for every single organ in her body, because she's sort of tiny and her head is just not big enough to fit that much smartness in. Although I'm not sure what being that smart can get you.

Sally was Isabella's partner for a long time, but then they got switched. Of course now she's Angeline's partner, so I'm sure Angeline never has to do any work. Which, added to the whole being loaded thing, really kind of bites.

BLAH BLAH BLAH

BLAH BLAH BLAH

SALLY LISTENS

Isabella talked too much and Palmer switched them

For now my lab partner is Isabella — whose head is plenty big — but there's a chance she's using part of it for a lunch box or laundry hamper. She has been conducting this top secret science experiment involving collecting every single one of those perfume sample cards that they put in magazines, and combining them into one massive **SUPERFRAGRANCE** that she says will smell as good as every known good smell in the Universe, combined. She has been doing this in science class because she already has about seventy of them crammed in an old baby food jar she's kept hidden in a cabinet in the science room. Just taking the lid off the thing to stuff another one in requires her to wear the science class safety glasses.

Isabella has been having a sinus problem, so she can hardly smell at all. But without the glasses, she says the vapor could still blind her for life.

Angeline and her genius partner, Sally, spotted us doing a perfume deposit today. Angeline, though beautiful and therefore fundamentally evil, didn't tattle. Call her **conceited.** Call her **stuck-up.** Call her **self-centered.** I mean it. Somebody go get the phone and call her.

But the truth is that she could have squealed but didn't. My theory is that at Angeline's lofty level of **MEGA-POPULARITY**, a snitcher is frowned upon. (At one point I thought I might have even seen her smile a little, but I've seen crocodiles do the same thing, so I can't be sure what it means.)

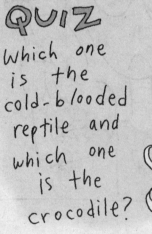

QUIZ
which one is the cold-blooded reptile and which one is the crocodile?

Tuesday 10

Dear Dumb Diary,

Isabella's sinus problem is still bugging her. She can't smell **anything**. She says her sinuses are bad enough that she could park in handicapped spaces if she were old enough to drive. Since she isn't, she says that the law allows her to just stand in them.

Wednesday 11

Dear Dumb Diary,

Isabella needed to make another perfume deposit today. I stood in front of her so that Mrs. Palmer, the science teacher, couldn't see what we were doing. (Mrs. Palmer replaced our previous teacher, Mr. Tweeds, who fell and broke his hip, which is what all old people do sooner or later because their skeletons are as brittle and cracky as pretzel rods. He's like 48 or something.) But it turns out that Mrs. Palmer, like most adults, doesn't really care **exactly** what you're doing when you are doing something that you're trying to hide. (Adults are like frogs that snap bugs out of the air without first getting a good look at them: Could be a butterfly. Could be a killer bee.) So Mrs. Palmer just separated us as lab partners.

Mrs. Palmer believes that switching partners whenever there is a problem is a good idea. Until today, I never believed her.

Mrs. Palmer is a teacher so naturally I assumed she would never do anything good for me. But...

You know how I said that adults are like frogs? Here's another aspect of their froggishness: Frogs are sometimes princes deep down inside. Or princesses, in Mrs. Palmer's case. (Although this particular princess would need a queen-size throne for **Her Royal Hineyness**.)

Mrs. Palmer had to split up another set of lab partners in order to separate Isabella and me. Sure, she *could* have paired me up with Margaret Parker, total reject. But she didn't. Dear, sweet Mrs. Palmer presented to me, like a humongous plate of cookies, my new lab partner, **HUDSON RIVERS**. She gave Hudson's old partner, Margaret Parker, to Isabella, like a plate of wet socks.

Don't get me wrong, Dumb Diary, Margaret is okay, I guess. She's kind of nice, but she's a **pencil chewer,** and most non-beavers find that a bit repulsive. (Isabella says that Margaret is a **"GERD,"** which is a **GIRL NERD.**)

Isabella's Terms for Girls

GERD
(GIRL NERD)

MORONICA
(FEMALE IDIOT)

CHOCK
(chick jock)

COW
(WOMAN BULL)

Isabella used the opportunity to share with me *(again)* more about her theories on Popularity. She says that Unpopularity is contagious, and you can catch it the same way you catch the **Flu** or **Bad Dancing.** Honestly, though, I don't believe that Unpopularity is a real Force of Nature, like Gravity or Deliciousness. I told her that she should be more open-minded about her new partner. And that deep down inside, Margaret is probably a good person.

Then I realized what a beautiful and sensitive thing I had said, and I imagined that maybe one day I might open a big sanctuary where all the **Social Rejects** could live and run free and never have to worry about wedgies again. Plus, I could sell tickets to people to come and look at them.

Little Billy feeds one of my captive rejects its favorite snack

Thursday 12, 3:45 AM

Dear Dumb Diary,

    I can't believe I stayed up this late. It's like, the middle of the night. There was this scary movie on TV tonight about this little girl who finds this old doll that's haunted, which anybody could tell was going to be haunted because she was a really sweet girl, and she really loved the doll, and there is just no way a movie is going to let a sweet little girl be happy with her doll. Not if it's a good movie, anyway.

    But now I am in serious trouble because I still have science homework to finish and I blame my mom who is the one who let me have this TV in my room after I begged two years nonstop for it. (I mean, a kid can't spoil herself, Dumb Diary, am I right? My spoilage is Mom's fault.)

    I'd like to write more, but I'm really tired and I have to get this homework finished.

If I don't, Mrs. Palmer
is going to bite my

Friday 13

Dear Dumb Diary,

That's right. I fell asleep last night without finishing my science homework. Which means, as predicted, that Mrs. Palmer bit my head off. And then it got worse. Figuring that the problem was with the new lab partner arrangement, she switched Hudson with Margaret. Now Margaret is my lab partner, and Isabella has Hudson.

Symptoms of Hudson Withdrawal (exhibited ONLY in private)

And since I missed the homework, Mrs. Palmer suggested that Margaret and I get together over the weekend to get me caught up. And Margaret said, right there in front of many Popular ears, between munchy chomps on a damp pencil, "Great. What time should I come over, Jamie?"

If I had been less tired, and outfitted in more confident clothing (thanks, Stinker), I might have come up with a cool comeback. Maybe the coolest one ever, but now we'll never know because I sleepily said, "whenever," and Mike Pinsetti, who used to be in the business of making up nicknames for people, but is currently experimenting with other forms of annoying harassment, made a loud kissy-kissy sound. As most people know, in some parts of the world, the kissy-kissy sound of a bully is enough to actually legally marry two people to each other.

Kissy Kissy
smoochy
smerchy
kissy

In this case, it suggested that perhaps Margaret and I were now best friends, and I could feel the Popularity flying off me like the delicate petals of a beautiful flower that somebody had stuck into the spinning blades of a fan.

Afterward, of course, Isabella didn't miss the opportunity to point out that I should be more open-minded about my new lab partner. I told her that open-minded is what you are if you get hit in the head with an ax, and I felt plenty open-minded enough.

Anyway, Dumb Diary, Margaret is coming over tomorrow.

Saturday 14

Dear Dumb Diary,

As foretold, Margaret came over. We finished the homework junk, and I realized that even though at first I had thought that Margaret was sort of an Unpopular Goof, after I got to know her a little, I realized that deep down, she was much worse than that.

often the inner person is way grosser

If there was anything to this Unpopularity infection thing, I was in serious trouble.

Fortunately, Isabella stopped by and we had a minute to talk privately while Margaret was in the bathroom, doing whatever it is that Unpopular people do in there. (Make themselves LESS presentable?)

The secret products of The UNPOPULAR

Pork-color contact lenses

Isabella had stopped by out of concern. She was concerned about her jar of SuperFragrance, which was gone, probably found by Mrs. Palmer. She was concerned that her lab partnership with Hudson didn't bother me enough. I assured her that it did, but since she was my best friend, I decided not to dwell on it. And she was most concerned that Margaret could drag down my Popularity, and since I'm friends with Isabella, it could affect her Popularity as well.

But Isabella had the solution. . . .

And it was an excellent one:
A MAKEOVER.

MAKEOVER PATIENT
PRIOR TO PROCEDURES

HUMP REMOVAL AND RELOCATION

FULL BODY SHAVE

NOSE JOB

TAIL REMOVAL

EARS MOVED

NEW HAIR AND MAKEUP

PERFUME

HUMPS SEWN BACK ON

GLAMOROUS WARDROBE

EXPENSIVE SHOES

SPINE STRAIGHTENED

See? Makeovers totally work!

Just like on TV. We will help Margaret fix
herself up a little, and thereby undo whatever
damage she has done to us. Like all of our plans,
this is surely a great idea.

Other great ideas of ours

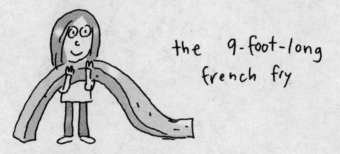

the 9-foot-long
french fry

some kind of pill you
could take and be
instantly healthy

the 18-foot-long
french fry

I was trying to figure out a delicate way to suggest the makeover, but Isabella had already come up with a gentle way to introduce the idea to Margaret.

Margaret did not take this as hard as you might think. She seemed kind of sickly grateful for the attention. I felt a little bad and might have pulled out right there, except for how much fun it is to put makeup on somebody else's face. Tomorrow, Isabella and I, **Known Experts on Fashion**, will begin **PROJECT MARGARET.**

My Incredible Makeup Skills at Work

Frankenstein

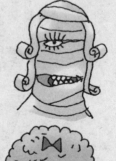

The Mummy

Wolfman

Sunday 15

Dear Dumb Diary,

Project Margaret begins.
Amazingly, Mom was totally okay with taking us all to the mall today. I was fully prepared for a huge argument, followed by some crying, an apology, and finally, a trip to the mall. Mom's saying yes right away saved me about four minutes.

I had saved up a LOT, too.

On the way to the mall, we passed the park, and saw Angeline again. But this time the kids looked entirely different from before. Obviously, her plastic surgeon dad had already started cutting the kids up to make perfect little miniature Angelines out of them.

Angeline's sick joy

Here's How those kids looked Before

Here's How they look now

We took Margaret around to the best stores at the mall. It was a little bit spiritual, because Margaret had not even heard of a lot of them. Isabella and I felt a little bit like we were doing something profound and wonderful, like teaching a gorilla sign language.

MARGARET LIKE MALL

Margaret started to chicken out a little at the clothes and accessories that Isabella and I had selected. She was craving some pencils pretty badly, but finally, she caved because we used **Peer Pressure** against her.

Bet I know what Margaret was thinking of

Adults think that Peer Pressure can influence what kids do, but it's actually a thousand times more powerful than that.

Obi-Wan Kenobi's Jedi mind tricks have nothing on Peer Pressure. Seriously. Isabella and I could have had Darth Vader in a miniskirt and braids in about five minutes.

We dropped Margaret off at Sally Winthorpe's house after the mall. I guess Sally had asked her over or something. (Maybe a Big Pencil Dinner.) But who cares? Because the main thing of the day or, as French people call it, *le main ting of ze day,* was **MY** new jeans! When we were at the mall, Mom found me a pair of **Bellazure Jeans.** They are the coolest jeans ever made and she bought them for me without my even having to ask. **Why did Mom buy me these really cool and really expensive pants??** I may never know.

But who cares?

The utter rapture of brand-
new jeans

Yeah, yeah. Mission accomplished with Margaret. She'll probably be a little bit better off. But now *I* own the coolest pair of jeans ever.

Stinker, I hope you are reading this, because I want you to know that an enraged girl can pick up a beagle by his fat little tail and hurl him directly into the core of the Sun if she is sufficiently antagonized, pants-wise.

So long,
Munchy

Monday 16

Dear Dumb Diary,

    I wore my new jeans to school today, and I felt like I was the most beautiful bottom-half-of-a-girl on Earth. I was just getting ready to drink up all the compliments when Margaret walked into science class.

Aren't
I
adorable?

Then I heard something that I had never heard before. It's not a sound you often hear. It was sort of a soft, wet, popping sound. I realize now that it was the sound of twenty-six jaws dropping open at exactly the same time.

Margaret was, well, she was **GORGEOUS.** Her hair, her perfume, her jewelry, her new clothes, were working together like a symphony orchestra comprised of the rare supermodels who are smart enough to read music.

Margaret

Isabella and I took a little bit of pride in it, feeling sort of like the people who own those incredible dogs at dog shows. You know what I mean: We're not the dog, but without us the dog would be licking a fire hydrant somewhere instead of looking like a million bucks. (That's SEVEN million bucks in dog money.)

Note: Nobody is currently prepared to accuse Margaret of this sort of fire hydrant lickage.

Margaret was so happy. And Isabella was happy. And I was happy. And Hudson was happy. *(grrr!)*

And okay, I wasn't. There was something vaguely sinister in the air, and I'm not sure what it was.

Tuesday 17

Dear Dumb Diary,

Here's a peculiar scientific phenomenon I learned in class today and, like all of the important scientific discoveries, it involves choosing your deodorant wisely.

For instance, these choices not so good

Margaret borrowed my pencil today. She must have forgotten that she was no longer a Gerd, because when I looked up she had it in her mouth and was enjoying what could only be described as a *relationship* with it. It was one of those moments when you find yourself looking around for something to hit somebody with. (I have this moment about fifteen times a day.)

But then this soothing breeze of fragrant excellence comes wafting off Margaret and I felt, like, soothed. That is one excellent deodorant. I even let her keep eating my pencil.

But the soothery didn't last forever. Is soothery a word? Whatever. By lunch I was no longer soothed. And Isabella was visibly shaken.

Sure, she's always visibly shaken, but today, she was picking up a really strange vibe. Bad Mojo. Evil Juju.

Isabella, who is sharply attuned to this sort of thing, walked in and instantly observed that the precarious **Lunch Table Dynamic** had been upset.

She said that some of the Medium-Popular kids were sitting with the Less-Than-Medium-Popular kids. For a moment I thought she was nuts, until I saw Margaret was sitting at **THE ULTRA-MEGA-POPULAR** table. Isabella said this really should not happen. For Margaret to escalate that quickly, it could destroy the Natural Order of the Universe, and worse. . . .

ISABELLA FREAKS

Isabella said that it meant that we had fallen a notch. By accidentally inserting Margaret in at such a high level of popularity, we had actually pushed everybody below her down. She said we're suddenly tumbling into the Pit of Zero Popularity. Can she be right? Is there really such a thing as Popularity, or is it all some sort of weird scientific theory?

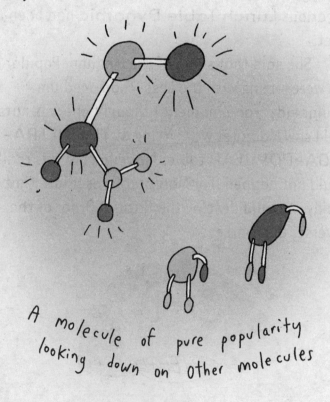

A molecule of pure popularity looking down on other molecules

Wednesday 18

Dear Dumb Diary,

Wore the New Pants again. I didn't wear them yesterday, of course. You can't wear them **every** day, or people will say you only have one cool pair of pants, which they would be jerks for being right about.

Thankfully, Stinker had not gone mental on them, but I don't know if that's because we are friends again, or because I've been hanging them in my closet where stubby little beagle legs can't reach.

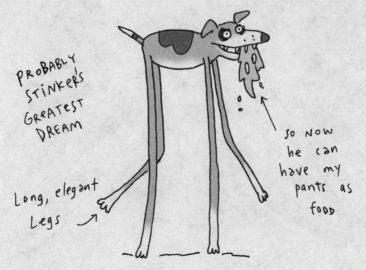

PROBABLY STINKER'S GREATEST DREAM

Long, elegant Legs

So now he can have my pants as food

Isabella and I may have destroyed **The Entire Universe.** (I, for one, do not believe the Universe should be this fragile, because it's where I keep all my stuff.)

But here's what makes me think we destroyed it. Today at lunch, somebody was missing at the Mega-Popular table. Isabella was right. We did such a magnificent job on Margaret's makeover that she has bumped everybody. She has even bumped . . . Angeline!

It was a truly beautiful moment. **Angeline had been taken down a notch!** It was the most beautiful lunchtime moment since the time Miss Bruntford, the cafeteria monitor, slipped on a smear of creamed corn and gave an involuntary figure skating performance that ended with a double axel into a face-plant.

I love figure skating

But, just like *that* beautiful moment —
which was shattered by our having to stare at
Miss Bruntford's massive underpants until the
paramedics arrived (You're not allowed to move
somebody in that condition. We also learned
that tossing Tater Tots at her wasn't a good idea,
either.) — *this* beautiful moment was shattered by
the realization that if Angeline had been demoted,
then we were even lower than we thought.

TOWER OF POPULARITY

MOVIE STARS
CHIP
MARGARET
ANGELINE
HUDSON
ME
ISABELLA
SALLY
PICKERS OF NOSES

When we
accidentally stuffed
Margaret in here
we destroyed
the Universe
and more
importANT,
LoweReD ouR
popULARITY

And Angeline was, in her typical deceptive way, not acting like it bothered her.

The pit of UNPOPULARITY

As we were standing there alternately blaming each other for making over Margaret in the first place, we noticed Hudson walking over to the Mid-Popular table and, just as he did, my pants — How can I put this? — decided to *join the conversation.* You get my drift, Dumb Diary? My pants cut the cheese. Let one fly. Baked a batch of brownies. Got the picture?

I know what you're thinking, Dumb Diary, pants can't get gas. And yet . . .

Fortunately for me, Isabella, who comes from a large family and is therefore an expert on swiftly blaming others, pretended to be horrified by some confused innocent kid nearby. She made Hudson think that the noise came from **Confused Innocent Kid,** or **Stinkypants,** as I have learned since lunch that he has come to be called. By everyone.

Of course, I admire Isabella for being so good at getting others in trouble, but she didn't believe me when I told her that it was the pants all by themselves, and not me.

STINKY PANTS

ISABELLA'S Big family has taught her how to efficiently ruin the lives of others swiftly

Families are the Best!

There's no **WAY** Isabella would have believed that the pants actually made me walk past the Mega-Popular Table, and that they also made me bump the table a little bit as if I was some sort of angry tough kid looking for trouble. Although now that I think about it, there's that one kid who actually bumps into *everything,* including lunch tables, and he's never looking for anything except his hat, which is routinely hidden from him.

What is with these pants, anyway?

Can PANTS make peopLe think you are a huge DERF, like BUMP-into-everything KID?

Thursday 19

Dear Dumb Diary,

    So tell me, Dumb Diary, if you were something small and ghastly, like a tiny, hairy creature that lived in a shower drain, and two beautiful fairy princesses took the time out from their very busy schedules to transform you into some sort of flying sparkling unicorn with diamond hooves that could shoot rainbow butterflies out its ears, would you just decide to throw it all away and cram yourself back into the shower drain?

HORRIBLE
thing
Re-crams
itself

Well, that is exactly what Margaret did. She showed up today in science class without the new clothes, without the new jewelry, without the makeup.

ugly old hair

ugly old hair accessory

ugly old clothes

ugly old beaver impersonation

ugly old shoe

ugly old other shoe

Isabella and I were floored. This meant that everything was back to normal. I accidentally let out this big cheer, and Mrs. Palmer dropped an alcohol burner, and then the whole room smelled like that substitute teacher who got fired last month for falling asleep in class.

Other Famous Substitute Teachers

— Mr. Stupid McClueless

The Sugar Substitute

The Tuna Sub

Of course, Mrs. Palmer employed her strategy of switching lab partners around. This means that now my lab partner is Mike Pinsetti, and Margaret is partnered up with some other kid, I forget who.

But I was so happy about Margaret's terrible judgment that this new partnerfication didn't really sink in.

In fact, as we switched seats, I even smiled at Mike Pinsetti, which made him try to smile back (*I think*), but it looked more like he had his hand caught in a car door. I may be the first person who has ever smiled directly at Mike's face.

Yes, indeed, everything seemed pretty wonderful until lunch. That's when we saw **IT**.

PINSETTI TRIES TO PERFORM SMILING

Margaret was sitting at the Mega-Popular table, talking to Chip, in her old, pencil-eating-shower-drain-creature form. Even Sally Winthorpe seemed to take notice. It was as though the very **Wonderbread of Reality** had been besmeared by the Peanut Butter of Illusion, and further obscured by the Grape Jelly of — oh, I don't know, I'm trying to make it all relate to lunch.

The simple fact is that, according to Isabella, we're much, much lower on the Popularity scale now than ever before, since it appears that Margaret has ascended on her own *(yuck)* merits.

Friday 20

Dear Dumb Diary,

Isabella came over tonight. She had some movie she had rented. (It was called *Terror at Your Throat*.) We started watching it, and it was about a haunted necklace and how bad things happened to this family after they got it. During the movie, Isabella jumped up and screamed that the necklace was exactly like my pants, which made Stinker commit Urine. It was probably because he is not used to people screaming while he is fast asleep. Still, I had to spank him a little for it.

Anyway, Isabella said it wasn't the makeover that boosted Margaret's Popularity and forced us down. It was the pants. She said it wasn't my loud "yahoo" in science that got me switched again so that I'm science partners with Known Goon, Mike Pinsetti. It was the pants. And she said it wasn't me who had done **you-know-what** all over Hudson Rivers. **IT WAS THE PANTS.**

SUPERNATURAL EVIL

PLUS GAS

I pointed out that I hadn't exactly gassed all over him. A debate followed, but she was firm on this point: The pants were to blame. **THE PANTS ARE HAUNTED.**

STRANGE THINGS MY

WATCH 20-MINUTE COMMERCIAL ABOUT A CHICKEN ROASTER

TASTE KIWI SHAMPOO TO SEE if it's as good as it smells

CALL HUDSON AND HANG UP. THIRTY TIMES.

PANTS MADE ME DO

imagine TRAGIC event in which everybody I know dies and I have to carry on prettily.

STROKE Roof of mouth with toothbrush and cause four-hour tickle.

Right now, Isabella is calling her mom to get permission to sleep over. I don't think I want to be in my room alone with the pants all night, and we plan to drive the spirits away tomorrow.

Saturday 21

Dear Dumb Diary,

Isabella's first idea was to tear the pants to shreds. But I wanted to see if we could just drive the wicked spirits out of them without the rippage. I mean, c'mon. They *were* pretty cool pants after all.

Isabella's next idea was to use a Ouija board to contact the tormented ghosts in my pants, but I don't have a Ouija board, so we tried to do it with a Monopoly game. Sadly, we didn't really make much progress, except we decided to try to make charm bracelets with the dog and race car pieces.

More Glamorous Jewelry From Old Games

Lovely String of Pearls made from balls out of Hungry Hungry Hippos™ Game

Spooky Voodoo Necklace made from old Operation™ Game Bones

Pierced earrings made from Mr. Potato Head's™ Ears

I thought we should light candles and speak some sort of mystic chant. We're not really well-informed on chants, so we said the Pledge of Allegiance, which, though technically speaking is not a mystic chant, still sounds pretty creepy when you say it low and zombie-like in a dark room with flashlights. (Dad doesn't allow lit candles in my room, so we had to make do.)

Freaked ourselves out a little

Finally, we decided to just pound the evil out of the pants, and this took the form of laying the pants out in the backyard and stomping all over them in various evil-destroying karate-like moves. It occurred to us both at the exact same time just how dumb we looked, so we took them inside and stuffed them into the washing machine. They were torn up pretty good. Maybe all it will take now is a little sudsing.

The point when we thought we might not be banishing evil and we might be huge spazzes.

Sunday 22

Dear Dumb Diary,

We walked to Isabella's house this morning, and when we passed the park we saw Angeline again. It looked like her dad had Plastic-Surgeoned those little kids back to their original appearances. Why would somebody do that? You can't just scribble out a plastic surgery and start over.

Or can you?

Late-breaking Thoughts

Could there be another, simpler explanation? I asked Isabella, and she said no. She said that the most obvious answer was that Angeline's plastic-surgeon father was doing and undoing operations on her younger sisters in order to make them look like different kids on alternating weekends. Also, it appeared that he had some sort of way to change their heights.

START   CHANGED   CHANGED   CHANGED AGAIN
                        BACK

You have to hand it to Isabella. When she's right, she's right.

When I got home, I peeked in the washing machine and the pants were gone. Hmm . . . **Demon Pants** mysteriously vanished. The only reasonable thing to do was to run screaming upstairs to my room.

Other times when screaming is necessary...

Monster is chasing you and your high heels are too cute to abandon

Eaten by Ants

Gramps accidentally shoots a moon

Monday 23

Dear Dumb Diary,

THE PANTS ARE BACK. This morning when I woke up, there they were, hanging on a hanger, looking brand-new, and totally haunted. They had mysteriously healed themselves. Also, I think they were staring at me.

I moved slowly and carefully around the jeans and reached into my drawer for another pair, only to discover that Stinker had chewed one of his big round holes in my last pair of non-evil jeans.

No jeans left! I was so angry that I dropped everything and made a big sign. It says, "Have You Been Mean to Your Beagle Today?" in glitter. **GLITTER,** Stinker. That means I *really, really* mean it. People use glitter on signs only when they are dead serious. And I put it up on my wall where he could see it all the time.

GRIND
SMASH
CRAM
MASH

HAVE YOU
BEEN
MEAN
YOUR
BEAGLE
TODAY?

Before I left for school, I cut up four hot dogs (possibly Stinker's favorite food) and put them in Stinker's dish. Then after he got a good look at them, I threw them out in the yard so that Stinker could sit by the window all day and watch the neighbor's cats sit out there and eat his hot dogs.

Tuesday 24

Dear Dumb Diary,

    Margaret continues to travel in the Mega-Popular circle in spite of her undeniable Gerdness (or would it be Gerditude?). The Evil of the Pants is strong. Indeed, they are twisting the very fiber of our Universe. Up is down, left is right, over there is over there now (I'm pointing).

Haunted By the Demon Denim

Isabella says our only hope is plastic surgery. She says that if we can get Angeline's dad to do some work on us, we might be able to claw our way back out of the Unpopularity pit.

pit-clawing is just murder on the nails →

I suppose it only makes good sense that you can feel better about yourself by letting somebody cut up your face, but I'm not sure exactly how that works. Isabella assured me that if we don't like what Angeline's dad does, he can always change us back like he does on Angeline's ever-changing little sisters. I guess I should consider it.

I told Isabella to ask Sally Winthorpe what she thinks, since she had offered to help Isabella and Margaret with their science homework after school.

Isabella says that Plastic Surgery makes you Beautiful

I just noticed my "Be Mean to Your Beagle" sign again.

I took Stinker into the bathroom and weighed him on the scale and told him that he was twenty pounds overweight.

I really don't want to be mean to Stinker anymore, but he has to learn his lesson.

Have a seat, Tubby

Wednesday 25

Dear Dumb Diary,

The pants are stronger than we thought. Even wadded up in the bottom of my closet, they still exert a destructive force at school, and here's how:

Margaret and Isabella's science homework was **WRONG.** Sally is never wrong. The only explanation is evil, jinxed jeans. Mrs. Palmer, like always, did a partner switch, and this time she put Sally and Hudson together, which seemed to make Sally sort of happy. (If I didn't know better, I would swear she was crushing on him a little. Do smart girls do that? I have no idea.)

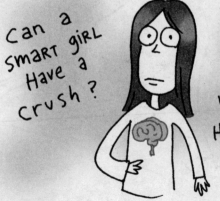

Can a smart girl Have a crush?

OR WOULD SHe Have a BRaiN WHeRe Her HeART SHOULD Be?

208

After school, Isabella made me help her corner Angeline. You are not going to believe how **WEIRD** this turned out to be, Dumb Diary.

Isabella is pretty blunt, so she just comes out and asks Angeline if her rich doctor dad will do plastic surgery on us.

Angeline looked pretty puzzled. She said that her dad worked in an office. He's an accountant.

I asked what about the little sisters we see her with in the park. Her dad keeps doing plastic surgery on them.

Those aren't her sisters. Those are kids she babysits. And they don't keep changing. They're different kids.

I know what you're thinking, Dumb Diary: Why does a rich girl need to babysit?

It turns out that Angeline is **NOT RICH.** She babysits because she needs to. She's saving up to buy — get this — a pair of Bellazure Jeans.

Angeline wants me to believe the lies I keep telling about her

But none of that is the weird part. Here's the weird part: Angeline and I wear the exact same size jeans. How can that be? She looks like a Greek statue, and I look like the place where somebody started to carve a girl and then gave up halfway through the project.

we wear the same size? I didn't know we were even the same species.

Isabella offered to sell Angeline my jeans at half price and Angeline said okay. (Not a big surprise, really, that Isabella would make that move. Once, Isabella tried to sell somebody my shoes, and I was wearing them at the time.)

I started to tell Angeline that they were possessed by some sort of horrible otherworldly force, and Isabella gave me an elbow in the ribs. I just had to tell Angeline after finding out she was my **size-sister**.

She didn't care. She said she didn't believe in otherworldly forces. It's your funeral, Angeline.

Otherwordly Garment Spookiness

HAUNTED PANTS
(I CAN PROVE THESE)

POSSESSED UNDERWEAR
(THESE SEEM LIKELY)

VOODOO MUUMUU,
(I HOPE THESE
EXIST. IT'S A
GOOD RHYME)

Thursday 26

Dear Dumb Diary,

What a day. What a day.

Mom came in and woke me up for school and noticed my anti-beagle sign. I explained to her what Stinker had been doing to my jeans, but that I was getting tired of being mean to him, anyway, and would probably take it down soon. I was thinking of replacing it with a gentler sign saying, "Be Mean to Your Beagle When He Deserves It." Also, I was planning to diminish the imposing threat of the message through the use of less glitter.

Mom may have noticed where a beagle's face was mushed into the sign

Then Mom dropped her bomb. Stinker had **NOT** made those holes.

After our little discussion about clothing a few weeks ago, Mom had decided to try to "get with it." She found out that the lighter-blue denim was the cool jean of the moment, and she looked through my magazines for tips on bleaching jeans. She couldn't find any, so she decided to just give it a whirl on her own.

I love my mom

But she's...

you know...

ALL

MOMMISH

She had spilled some bleach on my jeans the first time, and it turns out that bleach can eat a big round hole right through a pair of pants. She tried a couple more times, but those were not any better, you'll remember. She felt so bad she bought me the Bellazure Jeans.

Ah, **GUILT.** And some people say it's a bad thing.

Later, my mom found the Bellazure Jeans that Isabella and I had destroyed in the washing machine on Sunday. Not knowing that Isabella and I had attempted to stomp the Evil out of them, Mom assumed that SHE was responsible for wrecking them in the wash. She rushed to the mall and bought a brand-new pair, which she hung on a hanger in my room. (So they *didn't* mysteriously heal themselves.)

I looked over at Stinker, who was listening to all of this with what could only be described as a scowl, even though I'm not sure a dog *can* scowl with lips that are pretty much just flaps.

I wonder if dogs can hold a grudge.

Isabella's sinus problem cleared up. Why is that worth mentioning? The day got weirder. You'll see, Dumb Diary.

ISABELLA'S NOSE FINALLY DOES SOMETHING

In science class today, I noticed that Margaret seemed a little more, I don't know, Gerd-like.

I also noticed that Hudson and Sally Winthorpe, the brand-new lab partners, were really chatting it up. I mean, **BIG-TIME.** They were laughing and smiling, and it was like they were the only two people in the room.

HUDSON

SALLY

The evil of the pants is indeed powerful

Then Sally flashed a quick glance my way, and I saw something in her eyes: GUILT. I recognized it as exactly the same precise expression that Stinker had not had about the pants, but Mom had.

When Isabella passed by Sally, she stopped for a second, and I could tell she was confused by something. And it was more than Isabella's normal confused look.

SALLY

CONFUSED LOOK →

SCIENCE

Other normal confused looks

Science class was the same as ever: chemicals this and chemicals that. When the bell rang, I went out into the hall, and Angeline strolled up to me. She wanted the pants, and I pulled them out of my backpack and handed them to her. She dashed to the bathroom to try them on.

From inside the science room, I heard Isabella and Sally Winthorpe squawking about something. Then I heard a jar break, and the fire alarm went off.

Everybody in the whole school filed outside,
and Isabella dragged Sally over to talk to me.

Isabella is probably tough enough
to be a girl bully (A GULLY)

Isabella said, "I was right. Tell her, Sally."

And Sally Winthorpe, smartest girl in my grade (maybe the school) explained:

Sally had taken an interest in Isabella's **Top Secret SuperFragrance** project. She was the one who had taken Isabella's jarful of concentrated perfume samples. And she had done it for . . .

SALLY

DRAMATIZATION OF CRIME SCENE

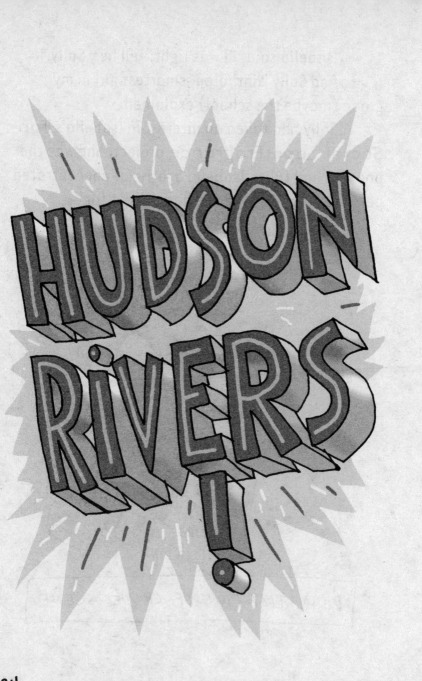

Sally had a crush on him. She had been convinced by discussions with Isabella that Isabella's theory of **Unseen Levels of Popularity** was right. Based on that hypothesis, Sally believed that she had to make room in the middle if she was ever going to be on the same level as Hudson.

EVIL GENIUSES LIKE SALLY ARE AFTER WORLD DOMINATION OR GUYS

So Sally used Isabella's powerful perfume concoction on Margaret by sneaking some into Margaret's backpack when she had gone over to her house to study. The **SuperFragrance** was so totally incredibly complex and enticing that it actually increased Margaret's Popularity, even after she abandoned the other makeover stuff and became the shower drain creature again.

That increase in Margaret's Popularity subsequently lowered Isabella's and mine.

CRUNCH CHEW

perfume Hidden in Backpack

MARGARET'S BEAVER-GIRL DROPPINGS

Then all Sally, evil homely genius, had to do was make sure that Isabella and Margaret did their homework wrong and hope that Hudson would wind up with her after one of Mrs. Palmer's predictable partner switches. And he did!

At that point, Sally started using the SuperFragrance on herself, thereby hypnotizing Hudson with the fragrance, which I had found so soothing that I let Margaret eat my pencil.

I was **not** amazed to learn how smart Sally is

I was amazed to learn that smartness is good for something

And she would have gotten away with it, too, if Isabella's sinuses hadn't cleared up. Isabella smelled the distinctive SuperFragrance as she passed Sally's desk. Right after class, Isabella jumped (Isabella said, "leaped like a cat," but I've seen her play volleyball. Trust me: I was being charitable when I said "jumped.") and snatched the jar out of Sally's backpack.

They fought over it, it fell and broke open, and Mrs. Palmer, overcome by the fumes, tripped the alarm, thinking it was some sort of chemical accident. (This would have been worth seeing. Like all girls from big families, Isabella is good at fighting. One time, when one of her big brothers was picking on her, Isabella slapped him so hard that he couldn't taste anything for three weeks. Sally never had a chance.)

It was a total Scooby-Doo moment. Except for the fact that my dog is sort of a reject, and we can't put Sally in jail. But we *are* meddling kids. You have to give us that.

Yup, it all felt pretty good until Hudson walked up and swept Sally away. She shot a glance back at us as if to say, "So what? I *still* got my way, and you're still on the bottom." And she was right. The entire Universe was still just plain wrong.

Behold the Scent of Evil

POOR DUMB HUDSON

which smells pretty good actually

And then, **IT happened.** I looked up and I saw Angeline coming out of the school. She had been changing in the bathroom when the fire alarm went off. Everybody in the school was outside. And when she opened the door, they all looked. It was the grandest entrance ever made, even though technically, it was an exit.

Angeline was wearing the Bellazure Jeans. But she was walking (I don't know how she does this) in slow motion. Even her hair was blowing in slow motion. Every eye in the school was glued on Angeline and the jeans and the knees of the jeans, which had holes in them.

← This is Beagle's work!

Stinker! These weren't Mom's perfect round bleach holes; these were the irregular holes gnawed by a mean little dog: rough, scraggly, thready holes. **WHY, STINKER? WHY?**

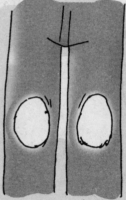

BLEACH HOLES

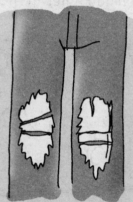

BEAGLE HOLES

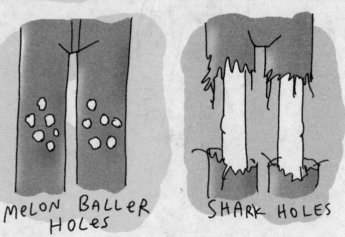

MELON BALLER
HOLES

SHARK HOLES

Suddenly, I understood why. It was clear to me that it was because I told Stinker he was twenty pounds overweight. In dog weight, that's **140 POUNDS.** No wonder he was angry. Nobody wants to be told that they are 140 pounds overweight. The jeans were ruined.

But then I saw — we all saw — Angeline's kneecaps peeking out through the openings. It turns out that her knees look more like little tiny perfect bald angel heads than knees.

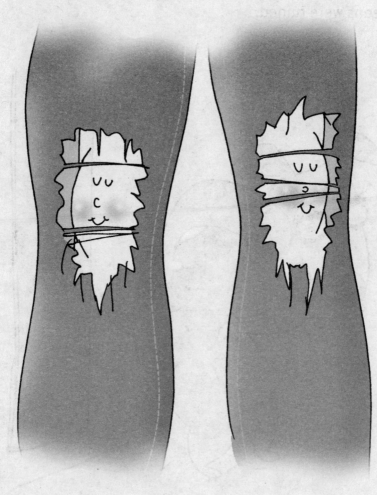

Angeline had just set a trend. Or maybe
Stinker had. Either way, fragrance suddenly meant
nothing to anyone. We all knew that how people
smelled didn't matter, as long as they had jeans
like Angeline's.

Angeline had regained her rightful position among the Mega-Populars. And Isabella said that it was like the spell of Margaret's makeover, the SuperFragrance, and the haunted pants had been broken.

Angeline walked over and handed me the money for the jeans. "I'll take 'em," she said.

And then Chip, King of Guys, and Hudson (who had abandoned Sally somewhere) walked up next to Angeline.

"Cool pants," Chip said.

Angeline looked right at me. A lot of things could have happened at that moment. She could have said almost anything.

What she did say was, "Thanks," pointing at Isabella and me. "These two designed 'em."

small feminine heart attacks

Friday 27

Dear Dumb Diary,

Science class was, well, quiet today. Half the kids had on torn jeans, except for Mike Pinsetti, who had torn the elbows out of his sweatshirt. (Not a bad try, for him.)

Isabella was more at peace than I've seen her in weeks. The pants had not been haunted, and the Universe seemed to be in balance again. The true Popularity Order had been restored. Also, Isabella

took some delight in pointing out that now it was absolutely clear that the pants themselves had not **Cut One** in front of Hudson.

It was me. (I blame Mom's cooking.)

Margaret was just happily enjoying pencil after pencil.

Sally didn't look quite so smart anymore, but Isabella and I decided to keep this to ourselves. Isabella says that we had a massive Popularity boost that brought us back up to normal, and maybe even slightly higher, thanks to Angeline. Besides, Sally was just after what we're all after.

Except for Angeline, who already has it.

Anyway, thanks for listening, Dumb Diary. I gotta go. I just remembered there's somebody I owe four hot dogs.

Jamie Kelly

THIS DIARY PROPERTY OF

Jamie Kelly

SCHOOL: Mackerel Middle School

Locker: 101

Best friend: Isabella

Destiny: Princess OR Spy/Ballerina

Pet: Beagle shaped thing

GREAT DANGER AWAITS
YE WHO READS FURTHER.

I'm serious.
Thou shalt be
CURSED if thou
reads further. And
you can tell I'm
serious because it
says *SHALT* and *thou*.

Dear Whoever Is Reading My Dumb Diary,

Are you sure you're supposed to be reading somebody else's diary? Have you done this before? If I did **NOT** give you permission, you had better stop right **NOW**.

If you are my parents, then **YES**, I know that I am not allowed to call people idiots and fools and turds and trolls and all that, but this is a diary, and I didn't actually "call" them anything. I *wrote* it. And, if you punish me for it, then I will know that you read my diary, which you do *not* have permission to do.

Now, by the power vested in me, I do promise that everything in this diary is true, or at least as true as I think it needs to be.

Signed,

Jamie Kelly

PS: Although if it's **You-know-who** that's reading my diary, well, then, it's totally okay. But if it's **You-know-who,** then you had better close this book right now, or else **You-know-who** is going to get a **you-know-what** in the **you-know-where.** You know?

PSS: I know that you don't believe in fairies or anything, so you probably wouldn't believe a fairy could turn you into a frog if you kept reading. But I'll bet you believe in hammers and I'll bet you believe that I have one and I'll bet you believe that I know where your head is. Let's just say that fairies are not your biggest worry if you decide to keep reading.

Saturday 31

Isabella was over for most of the day today and we worked out our entire future together. We're going to marry identical twins and live next door to each other and have exactly the same number of kids (nine girls, eight boys) and we'll time it so that they're all the same ages as each other's kids.

We'll have our own clothing store but we won't sell anything good to people we hate. Our husbands will be firemen or doctors or something, but they have to be the same thing so that neither one of us is richer than the other. And if one of our husbands gets in an accident and loses a foot or something, the other husband will have to cut his off just to be fair.

I really didn't think this was a reasonable thing to expect from a husband, especially if instead of getting a foot cut off it's something like falling out of an airplane. But Isabella says that she is much more of an expert on guys than I am, and that our husbands will be so totally into us that they will probably come up with this idea by themselves, anyway.

Sunday 01

Dear Dumb Diary,

Once again, Mom committed **Dinner** against the entire family tonight. As usual, I'm up here in my room clutching my guts wondering what the police would call this particular food crime. Maybe **Assault with a Breaded Weapon?** Or **Hamicide?**

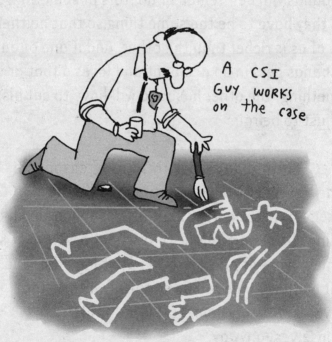

A CSI GUY WORKS on the case

I really don't know what kind of meat was in the **Meat Thing,** but I'm sure that Mom has a cookbook somewhere called *101 Recipes Using Ingredients That Shun the Daylight.*

Dad and I have been trying not to complain about the food because a few weeks ago, Mom had one of her Nobody-Appreciates-How-Hard-It-Is-to-Make-Dinner-and-One-Day-You'll-Appreciate-My-Cooking episodes. In retrospect, Dad and I probably should not have held our noses all the way through dinner.

Fortunately, I had the foresight to make a candy necklace out of Rolaids, so I can kind of medicate myself throughout the meals. Dad's not so lucky.

Mom might notice if Dad wore a Big Honking Necklace to Dinner

WARNING TO MY FUTURE CHILDREN: If I ever
have children and they are reading my diary right
now, I want you to know, kids, that you must never
ever ever eat Grandma's cooking. Also, My Little
Darlings, you are grounded for reading my diary, so
go find Mommy right now and tell her what you've
done, because you're in for a **HUGE** punishment.

And I'm telling Santa.

Children! Beware of Grandma's
Baked Uck!

Since it's Sunday, Dumb Diary, I have to work on the homework that's due tomorrow instead of sitting on the couch watching reruns of reality TV shows, which is what I'd really like to be doing. As Dad helpfully pointed out, if I had finished my h.w. on Friday, I could be relaxing right now. Dads are really good at pointing out *Things Everybody Already Knew.*

Anyway, we're finishing up our poetry unit in English class right now, and I have to write a poem about feelings. Here's what I have so far:

Mother dear, you've helped me grow
Into a pretty blossom.
So now I'd really like to know
Why you would feed me possum.

Monday 02

Dear Dumb Diary,

ANGELINE!!

Angeline rears her ugly head! Which of course isn't ugly, and I'm not even going to talk about her rears. You get the idea.

You remember last week how I told you that Isabella told me that Anika Martin, who is friends with Amy Feinstein (who we talk to sometimes even though she was born with the handicap of being a year younger than us), who is friends with a girl named Vanessa Something, who knows Angeline's cousin, told *her* that she had heard that Angeline had come up with a new top secret shampooing technique.

Supposedly, Angeline has invented something called **ZONE SHAMPOOING**. The idea is that you shampoo each zone of your head with its own distinct fragrance of shampoo. Anytime Angeline wants to, she can flip her hair in one direction or the other and shoot a delicious waft of fragrance right at your unsuspecting nose. More diabolical yet, she can sequence her hair flips and combine fragrances so that maybe you think you just smelled apple pie with vanilla cinnamon ice cream, or maybe a kiwi-strawberry smoothie with a touch of key lime.

Why would somebody want to do this evil thing?

MY THEORY OF THE EXCELLENT ODORS SHE PROBABLY HAS LOADED

RASPBERRY · BUTTERSCOTCH · LEMON-LIME · SUN-TAN LOTION · PIZZA · BABY'S HEAD · KIWI · SALAD · BUBBLE GUM · CANDY STORE

Well, Dumb Diary, I can tell you why somebody might **NOT** want to do this thing. Today I gave Zone Shampooing a try, and when I attempted to shoot Hudson Rivers (eighth-cutest boy in my grade) a snootful of Raspberry Delight (right side of head) combined with Coconut Madness (left lower quadrant of head), my English teacher, Mr. Evans—who was walking by at that exact moment—saw my attempt and thought I was having a seizure. He took me to the office, and the school nurse made me lie down on the cot for a while.

WHIP
WHIP
FLAIL
WHIP

seriously—why would somebody think this was a seizure?

Then, at lunch, Isabella admitted that maybe she didn't have the story straight and might have made some of it up. I don't really blame her, though — it sounds so much like something Angeline might do that if I had made it up myself, I probably would have believed it, too.

Other things Isabella can't remember if she really heard or just made up.

You can play a slice of Baloney in a DVD player.

Some perfume has whale vomit in it.

Here, we throw rice at weddings. In Japan, they throw hamburgers.

It is medically impossible to put on mascara with your mouth shut.

Tuesday 03

Dear Dumb Diary,

    I was the first person who had to read my poem out loud in Mr. Evans's class today. He liked it, I think, and he said something about something and then something else about something else, and I think he might have continued on about something else after that for a while, finishing up with something about something. I know that I am supposed to be paying better attention to Mr. Evans, but I was trying to watch Angeline out of the corner of my eye and didn't hear everything Mr. Evans said.

I was trying to watch Hudson at the same time out of the corner of my other eye, which, in fairness to Mr. Evans, probably **DID** look a little bit like I was having another seizure — kind of like the one I didn't have yesterday — and I was sent down to the office again for a little lie-down time on the cot.

Even though Mr. Evans was pretty sure I was going mental, he still made sure that I caught the next big assignment on the way out the door. Now that we're done with poetry, we have to select a popular fairy tale and write a report about it.

See, some teachers don't care if you're sick — they still make you do your work. I heard that one time this kid had one of his legs chopped off by a snow blower on the way to school, but since he had Mr. Evans, the kid dragged himself to school anyway, and Mr. Evans is so strict that he marked the kid *partially* absent.

FAIRY TALE ASSIGNMENT
1. PICK A FAIRY TALE.
2. HOW DOES IT APPLY TO YOUR LIFE?
3. I DON'T CARE IF YOU'RE DEAD. DO IT ANYWAY.

Wednesday 04

Dear Dumb Diary,

As you know, Dumb Diary (since I like to doodle on your face every day), art is one of my favorite subjects. But today in art class, Miss Anderson (the teacher who is pretty enough to be a waitress) said we're going to be doing a project involving photography, which, according to her, is art.

I think that's kind of like saying that recording a song is the same as singing one, but Miss Anderson is one of the few teachers I really really like, so I only performed a mild dirty look when she said it.

Miss Anderson Does not HAve to Be A teacher

She might even be pretty enough to be a shoe salesperson

Had I known that she was going to buddy me up with Angeline on the project, I would have used a much stronger dirty look. Possibly even *Dirty Look Number Eleven.*

(Note: It's important to practice your dirty looks and keep them numbered. Never try to mix them. Once I detonated numbers 8 and 4 at the same time, and it came out looking like a smile. It's a long story, but that accidental smile is why I unintentionally went with my aunt one time when she needed to shop for her big old bras.)

My Arsenal of Dirty Looks

1.
2.
3.
4.
5.
6.
7.
8.
9.
10.
11.

Our photo projects are going to go up in the lunchroom at the end of the month for the whole school to see. Angeline already had an idea for ours and, before talking it over with me, she just blurted it out in front of the entire class. That's right, Dumb Diary, She just "cuts the idea" the way some people cut farts.

Angeline suggested that she and I collect pictures of all the teachers when they were kids and make a big collage out of them so that everybody can see for themselves, I guess, just how punishing time is on the human body. Miss Anderson loved the idea, of course. As anybody can plainly see, she is beautiful now so she was for sure even more beautiful before she became a teacher (since there is no way that working with kids can improve your appearance).

So she told us to get started.

The woman who worked with kids

Day 1   Day 2

I know what you're thinking, Dumb Diary. You're thinking, **"Wow, Jamie. You're totally pretty and a really good dancer."** I'm not going to tell you you're wrong, Dumb Diary, but please, try to stay on the subject. There is more to this whole art class tragedy.

It's true my grooves are righteous

My so-called best friend, Isabella — who may be missing that part of the body where you keep your soul (It might be called the Soul Hole. I'm not a doctor.) — announces that *her* photography project is to put up pictures of everyone in the class with their pet, to show how people and their pets look alike.

"*PEOPLE AND THEIR PETS LOOK ALIKE,*" she says.

First off, my pet is a dog, which is the international symbol for **Ugly Girl**, and my dog is the dog that other dogs are grateful that they at least don't look as bad as.

I don't want to say that Stinker is ugly, but the only reason other dogs sniff him is to see which end is his face.

So, thanks a lot, Isabella.

PS: I tried to secretly sniff Angeline from two sides today to see if she really is Zone Shampooing. I couldn't tell the difference. I don't think there is such a thing.

PPS: There is, however, a way to creep somebody out by trying to smell both sides of their head.

Other ways I have creeped people out in the past

Tried to casually peer up Uncle's nose

tasted comb

mmm mmmm

was spotted practicing kissing on arm

Thursday 05

Dear Dumb Diary,

That's right. It's Thursday. And Thursday, at Mackerel Middle School and other penitentiaries, is traditionally **Meat Loaf Day.** That means it's also the day we traditionally get all sorts of grief from Miss Bruntford, the cafeteria monitor, for not finishing our meat loaf.

Today, I quietly mentioned that the people on *Fear Factor* wouldn't finish our meat loaf, either. Evidently, I said it loud enough for Miss Bruntford's houndlike ears to pick it up, because she came right over and said to me, "What? What is so terrible about this meat loaf?"

And then, Dumb Diary, she took a bite.

REEK REEK

Okay, here's the thing: I don't hate teachers. I actually like some of them. (One time, I even saw one at the mall and she was buying underwear such as actual people wear.)

But when Miss Bruntford took a bite of the meat loaf, and her mouth was filled with the flavor that many have described as a combination of a petting zoo in July and a burning bag of hair, well, I have to tell you, it was a beautiful, beautiful moment.

I'm not even sure how to describe it exactly. I think Miss Bruntford herself summed it up best when she said . . .

Friday 06

Dear Dumb Diary,

I'm not sure what happened to Miss Bruntford. She wasn't in school today, and there was something so pleasant about it all that I temporarily forgave Isabella for her stupid people-pet lookalike idea and we ate together at lunch. Isabella says she heard that Miss Bruntford is in the hospital with **Spontaneous Diverticulosis** or something. It's one of those old-people diseases that makes them talk about their bowels to others. She says we're getting a new cafeteria monitor next week.

The oldsters do love their intestinal chats

I never wished for Miss B. to get sick. At least, I never actually threw more than three bucks in quarters into a fountain when I wished I for it. But if she had to get sick, it really is sort of like an **Act of Justice** that it was the meat loaf that did her in.

It almost makes me believe that, in addition to fairies like the Tooth Fairy, there's a Fairy of Food Poisoning.

The Fairy of Food Poisoning

Brings Gut distress to the mean

The Ugly Fairy

Brings WARTHOGGISH Features to the Stuck-Up

The Flub Fairy

Brings flub to under Grandma's arms

Mike Pinsetti gurgled up to the table while Isabella and I were eating.

Mike Pinsetti, you might remember, is the official nicknamer of the school. He has some sort of evil talent for coming up with nicknames that sting and stick. Here are just a few of his creations:

Stinkerbell

Moldylocks

Pimplestiltskin

Anyway, I made the mistake of accidentally smiling at him once, and I'm afraid that now he is under the delusion that I think of him as, you know . . .

So Pinsetti is standing there with Isabella, and I'm just staring at him and I think he's trying to say something to me. But just as I went to perform **Dirty Look Number Four,** Angeline walks past and I'm sure she flipped a blast of weapons-grade **Raspberry Wonderfulness** directly at us from one of her many alleged Shampoo Zones.

Pinsetti and I are both momentarily stunned by the irresistible deliciousness of Angeline's attack and, against our will, we both sort of smile because — I mean, let's be real — you can't help but smile a little when you are awash in a cloud of **Raspberry Wonderfulness.**

So then, thanks to Angeline, Pinsetti and I are looking into each other's eyes while the bottom halves of our faces are smiling, and we are — I'm going to be sick — *sharing* this moment. And at the same time we're both trapped inside — I'm going to be even sicker — a fog of Angeline's stink.

Isabella said she could practically see **Pure Love** squirting out of Pinsetti's ears. I said it was for Angeline, but Isabella said it was for me. So don't be alarmed, Dumb Diary, if I wake up screaming several times throughout the night.

Saturday 07

Dear Dumb Diary,

    Saturdays are so cool that I will never ever figure out why they only made one of them per week. Here's my idea for a whole new lineup of days:

SATURDAY
I can't improve on Saturday so I'm not changing it.

SUNTURDAY
This will be another Saturday, but it will also have the aimless quality of a Sunday.

MONTURDAY
You can't get all your fun into just two Saturdays, so this is a bonus third.

WEEKSDAY
NOBODY LIKES WEEKDAYS. (THAT'S WHY THEY'RE CALLED "WEAK DAYS") LET'S GET THEM ALL OVER IN A SINGLE DAY.

FRIDAY
OK, IT'S A WEEKDAY BUT FRIDAYS ARE VERY IMPORTANT FOR PLANNING YOUR SATURDAYS.

FRIDAYNIGHTDAY
THIS IS AN ENTIRE DAY THAT'S NOTHING BUT FRIDAY NIGHT, ALL DAY LONG.

I called Isabella to see if she wanted to do something today, but her mom said she was at the mall with her dad. **I could hardly believe it!** Isabella has identified the five most embarrassing things a dad can do in public, and her dad does four of them:

DANCES

permits self to be witnessed in bathing suit.

DResses like Lady for Halloween

Talks

For the rest of the day, I was grabbing the phone every time it rang, figuring it was Isabella calling me back. Late in the afternoon, some woman who sounded familiar called for Mom, but I couldn't quite place the voice. Afterward, Mom was all excited but wouldn't tell me who it was or why she called. Some dumb Mom-thing, I'm sure, like they're going shopping for wind chimes or something.

OtheR DUMB ThiNGS MoMS HAvE

NEeD FoR BIRDBATHS

Delight over tiny decorative soaps you're not allowed to actually use

Infantile joy when using puppetish oven mitts

Sunday 08

Dear Dumb Diary,

Saturdays rule! But I really don't mind Sundays, either. They're sort of like Saturday's less popular and less attractive little sister. She tries to be as fun as her older sister, but she still has to keep reminding you that you have homework due tomorrow and you have nothing to wear and there's a good chance Dad will be hogging the TV all day.

if days were people...

Saturday   Sunday   Wednesday

When I went downstairs for breakfast this morning, Mom was bustling around the kitchen all giddy and dazed, and said I could have candy for breakfast if I would just go eat it in front of the TV.

For as long as I can remember, Mom has practiced this sort of Motherly Irresponsibility whenever she wanted me out of the way. One time, I walked in on her when she was trying to force her mombutt into an old miniskirt and she was so embarrassed, she told me I could go outside and throw apples at passing cars if I'd leave her alone.

I knew her judgment was way off on that one so I didn't take her up on it, but candy for breakfast seemed only mildly self-destructive. I accepted her terms and let her have her ridiculous secret kitchen time.

Later on, Mom was cooking up a storm. Like most storms, we anticipated great devastation in its wake. You'll recall that Mom has cooked up a few memorable storms in the past. . . .

Like the Lasagna Dad and I felt was made with ferret.

But here's the weird thing: She cooked it, but she never actually inflicted it upon us. We smelled her cooking, we heard her cooking. Stinker even took the customary precaution of hiding his dog dish. But for some reason, Mom just packed it all up in a Tupperware container, stuck it in the fridge, and ordered a pizza.

Believe me: Dad and I did not ask questions. That would be like reminding your executioner not to forget his ax tomorrow.

Monday 09

Dear Dumb Diary,

Today in English class, Mr. Evans started our unit on fairy tales. We're discussing a few old favorites in class in order to understand what he expects from us on our reports. He started with *Hansel and Gretel,* which is about this witch who wants to eat a couple of grimy brats even though her entire house is made out of candy. I said that she was probably trying to drop a few pounds: **Children are high protein, low carb.**

Then we discussed *Snow White,* and *Rapunzel* and *Little Red Riding Hood,* and when Mr. Evans asked us what we thought of these fairy tales, I said that it was coming through loud and clear that back in olden times, if you had a really weird dumb name, you were probably just waiting for something disastrous to happen to you. I mean, you never hear about *Jennifer and the Seven Dwarves* or *Steve and the Three Bears.* Mr. Evans probably agreed with me deep down, but he bulged his Big Ol' Ugly Head Vein at me a little, anyway.

Jennifer and the Seven Dwarves

Lunchtime, Dumb Diary, was really something interesting today. It was even more interesting than when the lunch ladies had that dispute that started with angry words over who looked better in their hairnet, and ended with paramedics siphoning cranberry sauce out of a semi-plugged lunch-lady esophagus. (Note: In these sorts of situations, always bet on the more massive lunch lady.)

As I said, the school has somebody filling in for Miss Bruntford while her organs are healing or whatever. His name is Mr. Prince ("Prince!" Couldn't you just die?) He's a student teacher, which is a person who will become a teacher unless something better occurs to them at the last minute.

He is older without being fully old yet, which means he probably shaves more than twice a week but still does not have hairy ears.

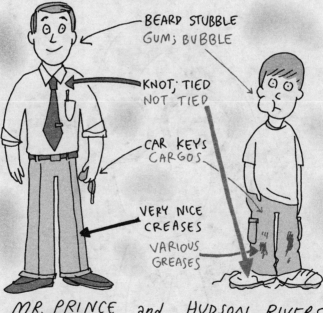

BEARD STUBBLE
GUM; BUBBLE

KNOT; TIED
NOT TIED

CAR KEYS
CARGOS

VERY NICE CREASES
VARIOUS GREASES

MR. PRINCE and HUDSON RIVERS
a comparison

Furthermore, Angeline walked right past Mr. Prince (Possibly firing Zone after scented Zone at him? It remains a theory.) and he did not even look at her, which I think is evidence that he is not into that whole gorgeous-with-excellently-perfect-blond-hair thing. But who can blame him? Nobody really cares.

Isabella said he is probably into dark-haired girls with round glasses, and I had to remind her that I don't wear glasses.

But Isabella was impolitely hinting that Mr. Prince would like her better than me, which is pretty rude since I had already started thinking he would like me better than her, and I felt like I had to tell her so and also execute a mild version of **Dirty Look Number Three.** Plus, I may have pointed out how her head is almost a perfect sphere, and she is **NOT** at all secure about her cranial roundness.

DiRTY LOOK NUMBER 3

MILD　　REGULAR　　EXTRA CRISPY

This turned out to be a pretty bad idea since — and I have shared this with you before, Dumb Diary — Isabella has older brothers, which means she is very good at all forms of fighting.

Isabella stood up in the middle of the cafeteria, smiled at me and said, with perfect sinister cruelty: "Let's see how he likes you when he sees your picture hanging up in the cafeteria side-by-side with your dumpy little beagle."

When I got home, I took a good hard look at Stinker. He's too old and fat to run any more, and he does not hesitate to express a sudden and extreme interest in his own body parts even when he knows you're right there in the room having a conversation with him. I can't stand the idea of being compared to him.

I'm going to have to sweet-talk Isabella out of this project.

MORBIDLY
SMELLY

MORBIDLY
OBESE

MORBIDLY
SENILE

MORBIDLY
WILLING TO
TASTE ANY
PART OF ANY
DOG ANY TIME

My Dog, Stinker

Tuesday 10

Dear Dumb Diary,

Okay, you can't sweet-talk Isabella out of anything. I explained to her today that I'm going to be totally embarrassed and humiliated when her project gets hung up, and instead of understanding and agreeing to scrap the whole idea like a best friend should, Isabella pretended to cry and said I was criticizing her art project.

When somebody actually pretends to cry as good as Isabella can pretend, and they really very nearly appear sad, you just have to back off.

In my defense, Isabella's pretend crying is better than most people's real crying, a skill she likely perfected to get her older brothers in trouble.

man, she's good

I thought about asking Isabella over for dinner, to take another crack at changing her mind, but Isabella, like all of my friends, sort of doesn't know how to interpret a dinner invitation. Everybody is aware of my mom's cooking challenges, even the teachers.

It's like if you were Dracula's kid and you asked somebody over for a neck massage.

None of this really matters much, because I had a long conversation over lunch today with Mr. Prince. **(Couldn't You Just Die?)**

It happened as I was taking my tray to the trash. I had done a particularly thorough job of abusing my leftover food today. I had shoved the macaroni and cheese into a large wad, stuck a carrot stick straight up in it, and dumped chocolate milk over the whole thing.

Mr. Prince **(C.Y.J.D.?)** was standing by the trash, and when I went to slide it in, he looked at it and said, "That a model of the Eiffel Tower?" and kind of laughed a little.

"*Sí,*" I said, not wanting to miss out on his reference to All Things French. And then I threw my garbage in the can and ran away.

Okay, Dumb Diary, I know. I know. Strictly speaking, "sí" is not exactly French for "yes." It's Spanish. But Spain and France are sort of the same big CountryOverThere and I was a bit flustered that he wanted to have a long conversation with me. Besides, I'm confident he knows that, even though I didn't actually speak French, I implied French.

It was a moment, Dumb Diary. We shared a moment.

Some French I think I Know

La Derriere

La Beret

La Brador
au La Vatory

Wednesday 11

Dear Dumb Diary,

Art class today. Angeline has collected almost half of the teacher's childhood pictures already. I did my part of the project by pasting them to the poster board and writing the teacher's name underneath each one.

I noticed that the really ugly teachers gave pictures of themselves as little kids, before the Ugly reached its advanced stages.

I'm also photographing some of the teachers. I try to catch them burping or something.

BWWURF

Miss Anderson's picture just happens to be from when she was about seventeen and a half. She just happened to be at the beach and she just happened to be in an adorable pose. I have seen so many pictures of these adorable poses that I'm starting to think that really pretty girls stay in these poses all the time, just in case somebody whips out a camera.

The Adorable Poser

← posing for a picture

telling the pharmacist about a sore on her back ←

mopping up cat barf in the basement →

Miss Anderson reminded us that we all had to get in our pictures for Isabella's project and that if somebody doesn't have a pet, they could just give Isabella a picture of an animal they resemble.

Of course, I saw my opportunity here, and after dinner I encouraged Stinker to run away from home. I might have gotten away with it except that the neighbors across the street called my parents to report that I had left the front door open and that I had thrown about twelve dollars worth of pork chops across the street onto their lawn.

Seriously. "Why *wouldn't* a fat ugly beagle chase after twelve dollars worth of pork chops?" I screamed as I picked up the raw chops and put them in a trash bag, out in the rain, alone in the dark. The neighbors watched me from behind their curtains like the timid, tattletaling turds they are.

Anyway, now that I think about it, even if Stinker had run away from home, he might only be gone three or four days. He's done it before, and that's usually how long it takes before he decides to come back.

Thursday 12

Dear Dumb Diary,

Mr. Evans had to remind us again today that our fairy-tale report is due in a couple of weeks. Then we read a few more fairy tales and talked about them.

We started with *The Princess and the Pea*, which is probably the most exciting and thrilling story ever written about somebody having mild insomnia. I said that it teaches us that you probably don't want to sleep in a bed that somebody has pead.

This **sounds** a lot different than it looks when you write it, but I think Mr. Evans cut me some slack because now he thinks I have seizures.

Hey, Dumb D, here's something new: This was the first Thursday since I've been at Mackerel Middle School when we were not forcibly meatloafed. We were all sort of mystified, but nobody was complaining.

And here is something else new (although it really shouldn't be). When I went to my locker today, somebody had romantically slid a note in through the odor vents.

I can hardly believe it! Here it is:

THE LOVE THAT CANNOT BE

A moment shared, a smile bright
As any smile can be,
So sad, yet so enchanting,
The Love that cannot be.
Signed,
m.P.

CAN YOU BELIEVE IT? "M.P." It's from <u>M</u>r. <u>P</u>rince! I would love to smash this note in Angeline's face and also smash it slightly lighter in Isabella's. It's **ME** that he noticed. Not Blondie, Not Sphere-Head. **ME!** And even though he knows that we can never be together — because I am normal-aged and he is old — he still needed to give his heart voice. How he must suffer and ache. I wonder if he yearned for me. This could be the first time I had caused a yearn. (Or is that **a "yearning"? "yearnfulness"? "yearnation"?**)

I showed the poem to Isabella and I think she may be a little jealous. I wonder if Mr. Prince would wait for me to grow up?

while waiting for you to grow up, a person should be allowed to read or listen quietly to the radio

Friday 13

Dear Dumb Diary,

I forgave Isabella again. It's amazing how just knowing that Mr. Prince wrote me a love poem makes me feel so confident. Isabella's meanness to me kind of dissolved away like blueberry stains on a denture commercial. (Note to old people: There are many other less inky pies to enjoy.)

Also, Isabella has very strong powers of persuasion.

Maybe somebody should invent toothpaste pie for denture wearers

I asked Isabella if she wanted to go to the mall with me this weekend, but she said she was going with her dad again. I quizzed her on this — complete with gagging noises — and she refused to talk about it. Isabella is up to something, Dumb Diary. I can tell.

Some of Isabella's Schemes

Tried to fly with Balloons. (first grade)

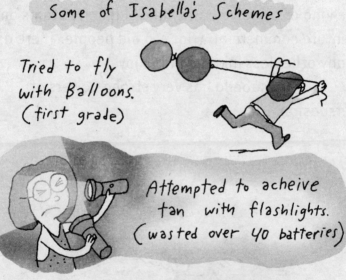

Attempted to acheive tan with flashlights. (wasted over 40 batteries)

Masqueraded as weathergirl to try to get principal to declare snow day in May.

I made another little garbage sculpture for Mr. Prince today. This one was a wadded-up lump of cheeseburger with some fries stuck in it to resemble the Statue of Liberty's head (in keeping with our cute French thing). Before I slid it into the trash can, I tried to direct Mr. Prince's attention to it with head nods and eyebrow twitches until I saw Mr. Evans coming at me with that **You're-Having-Another-Seizure** look in his eyes and I had to dump and run.

Mr. Prince and I are practically like Cinderella and Prince Charming except that, in our case, Cinderella is mutilating her food for attention and exhibits false seizure symptoms, and Prince Charming isn't all obsessed with footwear. But other than that . . .

Seriously, wouldn't it have been easier for the Prince to just recognize Cinderella's FACE?

I gave some more thought to helping Stinker run away from home this afternoon. After school, I made him watch a show on wolves on The Discovery Channel, hoping that maybe it would make him want to run wild and perhaps haul his chubby rump up some mountain and howl at the moon. But I don't think he understood.

Not even when I got a big round pillow and tried to make him howl at it by holding it over his face. I was only playing, but Stinker seemed to get a little panicky, and his wolf howl sounded a little like a whine.

He was so upset afterward that it took him, like, thirty minutes of constant gnawing on his chew toy (which I have named **Grossnasty**) to calm down.

I have no idea how I'm going to avoid giving Isabella a photo of Stinker.

Stinker goes freaky on Grossnasty

Late-Breaking News: Carryout tacos for dinner. Get this: Mom didn't have time to make dinner because she went to Miss Bruntford's house for a visit. MISS BRUNTFORD'S HOUSE!

Surprised, Dumb Diary? Me, too. I mean: A house?? I always assumed Miss Bruntford lived under a bridge, where she asked travelers riddles before she'd let them pass.

Since when would Mom visit Miss Bruntford?

Who cares. Dad and I don't want to ask too many questions. I ate so many tacos, my neck hurts. Note to Taco Company: Invent a taco that one may consume without suffering head dislocation.

Seriously, can you imagine trying to invent a brand-new food nowadays and telling people that there's one catch: You have to be sideways to eat it?

People are willing to endure SIDEWAYS-HEAD-EATING FOR tacos, but would they do it for

a sideways cheeseburger?

or

Sideways spaghetti?

TACOS REMAIN YOUR BEST BET FOR SIDEWAYS-HEAD-EATING.

Saturday 14

Dear Dumb Diary,

It's amazing. On school days, when I get up early, I'm so exhausted I can hardly walk, but when I get up early on a Saturday, I'm not even tired. How do your muscles know what day it is?

I walked over to Isabella's this morning. I figured that if I just **happened** to be there when she and her dad went to the mall, they'd have to take me along.

When I got to Isabella's house, unbelievably, right in the middle of her front lawn was this incredibly cute puffball of a kitten. I scooped it up and knocked on her door. When Isabella answered, I thought her eyes were going to pop out of her head.

"Where'd you get that cat?" she said, in one of those whispers where you're kind of yelling and whispering at the same time. I told her I found it on her lawn. She said that it belonged to one of the neighbors and they were looking for it and I had to give it to her to return to them. That was all fine with me, but I couldn't help noticing that Isabella was breathing just like Stinker did when I had him under the pillow during his wolf training.

Then she took the kitten and said the mall trip was cancelled, she'd call me later, and then *SLAM.* Just that fast, I had been de-kittened, de-malled, and blown off by my best friend.

When I was walking home, thinking about things I'd like to happen to Isabella, and trying to look sad (I'm rather pretty when I'm sad), I had that feeling you get when you're being watched. I looked up, and there, in a minivan — which was not the giant golden carriage drawn by the perfect white horses you might expect — was Angeline. And when we locked eyes, she waved. Not a big You're-My-Best-Friend wave, but not one of those weird upright rotations that the girls on parade floats do, either.

This in itself was odd, as Angeline and I are not friends because she is too beautiful and stuck-up to be a friend, but what was *really* odd was her mom . . .

Angeline's wave appeared almost human

I think this was the first time I had ever seen Angeline's mom, and I don't know what I would have expected, but it was not at all what I saw.

You know when a movie star brings one of her parents to an awards ceremony and you always think: Wow. Her parents are as ugly as mine. How did **THAT** happen?

That's kind of what it was like with Angeline's mom. Except not in the face.

Years ago, my folks and I were at the zoo, and a three-year-old, thinking he was looking at a porcupine or a sloth or something, tried to feed a peanut to the back of my head. It was at that moment that I knew I had **The World's Worst Hair.** That is, until now.

Angeline's mom had Angeline's beautiful face, but growing out in curly shiny sprouts here, and straight dry wisps there, her hair looked as though the stylist had misplaced her scissors and just tried chewing it off.

A handful of clips and ties and barrettes did nothing to improve things. It only made it look like she had stumbled into the display rack on her way out of the salon.

Angeline's Mom's shocking head

I believe that, somehow, while she was pregnant, the tiny, evil, infant Angeline spawn had totally sucked all the quality out of her mother's hair. I mean, what else could it be? Unless . . .

Unless this means that Angeline is going to grow up that way! Of course! Angeline is using up all of her **hairpretty** too soon. She's going to burn out.

As Angeline and her mom pulled away in their white minivan, I just stood there for a moment, confused and stunned . . . and happy. All I could think was that maybe, just like in fairy tales, **Dreams Really Do Come True.** Maybe there **IS** an Ugly Fairy, and one day, she will visit Angeline!

UGLY is so BEAUTIFUL when it happens to someone who Deserves it.

Sunday 15

Dear Dumb Diary,

It's Sunday and I figured I should start thinking about my fairy-tale report.

I've ruled out *The Pied Piper* since I don't buy kids following a flute player. A guitar, maybe, but not a flute.

I've also ruled out *The Emperor's New Clothes* because, well, simply put: **Ick.**

AND THUMBELINA IS KIND OF SCARY to me...

So I've decided to do my report on *The Frog Prince.* The story really speaks to me, because I'm practically identical to the Princess in the story except that I don't have a frog to kiss and make into a Prince, but I do have a Prince (Mr. Prince) who loves a place where they eat frogs (France). **Gross.**

Okay, okay. Strictly speaking, not everybody in France eats frogs. And they only eat the legs, anyway. And lots of gross people everywhere eat frog legs, not just gross French people. Leave me alone. It's a good comparison.

I'm sure that Angeline is doing her report on *Rapunzel*. I mean, how could she **NOT** do it on *Rapunzel*? Here are a few versions of Rapunzel I'd like to see Angeline star in:

The Prince is allergic to Rapunzel's shampoo and has to climb up her eyelashes instead.

prince is so fat that he pulls off Rapunzel's head.

Prince falls for a princess with brown hair of reasonable length. Rapunzel starves.

Monday 16

Dear Dumb Diary,

Another poem today from You-know-who!

> THE FAIREST BLOSSOM
>
> She is the fairest blossom. True,
> She blooms in any weather.
> But I must love her from afar.
> We'll never be together.
>
> Signed,
> M. P.

Can you believe the pain he's in? His suffering? The crushing heartache he endures every time he sees me?

God, it just makes me so happy!

Also, it's like a totally amazing coincidence that he wrote about me as a blossom after I did the same thing in my poem to my mom. It's like we share a common head. Isn't that sweet?

ok, a little creepy maybe

I showed this one to Isabella, and I think she may be even a little jealouser. Yeah, I'm pretty sure he'll wait for me to grow up.

Tuesday 17

Dear Dumb Diary,

    Today Mr. Evans told us that fairy tales were sometimes used to teach a lesson. He asked for examples and I said *Rumplestiltskin* taught an important lesson. (*Rumplestiltskin,* Dumb Diary, is the one about the creepy little guy who helps the imprisoned maiden spin gold from straw so she can escape a lifetime in jail, in exchange for her first-born baby.)

ew!

I said it taught us that pretty young maidens break deals all the time, even if you give them a mountain of gold and get them out of jail. If anything, I said, these pretty young maidens are the cause of all the trouble in the world, breaking into bears' houses and busting up their junk, antagonizing wolves, getting lost in the woods, making their stepmothers crazy. It goes on and on.

Mr. Evans's vein throbbed, and he said I was the first student that he had ever heard of rooting *for* Rumplestiltskin and **against** Red Riding *Hood,* which I thought might mean I was a genius.

But failing to cheer for the Goldilocks type is evidently a symptom of seizurism in Mr. Evans's book. So he sent me down to the nurse's office **AGAIN** for a little cot time. It's not a big deal anymore. The office ladies know me now and they just wave me in and I make myself comfortable. They even gave me my own key to the cot room this time and said that if I want different drapes in there or something, I can decorate it any way I want since I am the only one using it. This made them laugh at me a little, which made me say something like "old bats" or "old hags" or something like that. Anyway, I had to give the key back, and probably the drapes are out.

HAG BAT CRONE

Wednesday 18

Dear Dumb Diary,

    I found another poem in my locker this morning! !

> HEY, JAMIE, YOU ARE A CUTE GIRL,
> NOT THE TYPE THAT WOULD MAKE ME HURL.
> YOU'RE NOT AN OYSTER, YOU'RE A PEARL,
> YOU'RE CUTEST IN THE WHOLE WIDE WORL.
>
>   SIGNED,
>   SECRET ADMIRER

Okay. So maybe it's not his best work. Even Shakespeare probably had some off days.

But let's not forget the yearning. It probably hurts when he yearns, and that's probably throwing off his poetry. Shut up. He's calling himself an *admirer* now.

I wonder if there's a store where you can buy pedestals for your admirer to worship you on.

I returned his sentiments with a token of my affection that I presented in the form of artistically fingered food at lunch. I had captured The Sphinx quite well, considering how infrequently The Ancient Egyptians sculpted in spaghetti and Jell-O. Even Isabella agreed, and she says that since she is Italian, she is an expert on pasta.

There was also a pyramid but I ate it.

As I slid my love tribute into the garbage with a sad, slippery smush, Mr. Prince said that I had done a fabulous job and that, even covered in spaghetti sauce, my hands still looked like beautiful petite little doves that were bleeding badly (and at which somebody had thrown Jell-O).

He didn't exactly say that **mouthfully**. He said it more with his eyes. Or maybe I read his mind. I don't know. Anyway, when I turned around, Hudson was right behind me in line and he said "Hi," but since I'm sort of involved with Mr. Prince right now, I had taken a few steps before I even realized that Hudson had been speaking to me, so I didn't respond.

Angeline was right there, too, and she seemed a bit surprised. Maybe she was surprised by Mr. Prince's yearning. Or maybe she was surprised that I had blown off Hudson. Or maybe she was surprised to learn that The Sphinx would have looked better with a big meatball nose.

In any event, I'm sure I noticed her give her head a little forward flip, casting her hair fumes at poor unsuspecting Hudson, who I now think of as a child compared to my charming Mr. Prince.

Angeline looking confused.

Look how she even has to have pretty question marks in her head.

Thursday 19

Dear Dumb Diary,

    First thing this morning, I took another shot at Isabella. I tried to get her to let me say that I didn't have a pet, but she said that would undermine her integrity as an artist. I reminded her that last month she turned in a drawing she had done of Angelina Jolie for her self-portrait assignment.

    I asked her if I could just use a picture of a different beagle, like, one that was less of a disgusting slobber-mouthed odor museum than Stinker, but she said that would be dishonest. Then I reminded her that two months ago, she had drawn on her glasses with a marker in order to make everybody think she had blue eyes.

I asked her if she really believed that people look like their pets, and she said that it was not her but Science that had made this decision. I then reminded her that judging by the shape of her head, she must have a balloon for a pet.

Look! There's Isabella!

Which meant, of course, that we did not eat lunch together today.

At least there was no meat loaf for the second Thursday in a row, and no Miss Bruntford, either. I wonder if they've just decided to keep Mr. Prince on permanently. That would be excellently awesome, of course, although I suppose I should consider Mr. Prince's pain.

Okay, I considered it. It would still be excellently awesome.

While you wait for me to grow up...

You may __not__ DATE.

In fact, just stay indoors.

Try to stay up on fashion trends so when I show up you're not all 20-YEARS-AGO.

Spend time each day thinking about hair that is not blond. Or red. Or black. Or nice.

Friday 20

Dear Dumb Diary,

Angeline stopped by my locker this morning, and she had "our" art project almost completely finished, except that she wanted me to apply the glitter. No surprise, really. I'm known widely for my skills with glue and glitter, or **Glittifying,** as those of us in the biz like to call it.

Glittifying

Sequinization

emflowerment

Rhinestonery

Stickerating

Advanced Decorator at Work

Angeline had pictures of all the teachers when they were younger. Some were babies, some were teens. I have to admit, for a minute, it seemed like this **WAS** a pretty good idea.

But then I saw the picture labeled "Bruntford."

miss Bruntford ←

It looked like a kindergarten photo of a plain-looking little girl . . . who looked like me. And not just a little bit like me, Dumb Diary. She looked totally exactly **precisely** like me.

see the resemblance?

You know what this means? It means that if Miss Bruntford looked like **ME** when she was a kid, then I'm going to look like **HER** when I'm an adult!

NOW

BEFORE YOU KNOW IT

"Does it look okay?" Angeline said, all smuglike. "I hope you don't mind that I did the glitter myself. I'm going to drop it off with Miss Anderson now, so she can put it up in the cafeteria next week."

And then Angeline paused for just a second, with this strange kind of tiny smile that was as small and bewildering as a baby's butt.

I know that she noticed the resemblance in Miss Bruntford's photo and she wanted me to crumble.

But I didn't. I stayed strong and silent and just nodded okay, thinking that this was even worse than Isabella's project, and wondering why I had thought there was something bewildering about baby butts.

Next week, both Isabella's *and* Angeline's projects go up in the cafeteria, and everybody — including Mr. Prince — will see them.

I very much doubt that even *Rumplestiltskin* can save me now.

But maybe Humpty Dumpty could

Saturday 21

Dear Dumb Diary,

When I woke up this morning, I knew this might be my last chance to persuade Isabella to change her project. I hoped that when I told her about Baby Bruntford, she might take pity on me and change her mind. I was also fully prepared to lie and say her head was becoming less round. (When in reality, if anything, it's getting rounder.)

How Isabella should Bowl

When I got to Isabella's house, there on her front lawn was the kitten I found last week, along with another one. I scooped them up and rang the doorbell. Isabella was holding a third, much younger kitten in her arms when she opened the door. When she saw me standing there with the other two kittens, she looked just like she did after we learned about **you-know-what** in biology.

"Oh, good," she lied.

Isabella can lie to almost anybody but me. I can always spot her deceptions, and she usually doesn't bother even trying. The fact that she was even trying indicated that she was really and truly desperate.

"My neighbors lost those two kittens that you have there, as well as this third kitten, which I found just before you got here. Let me have them all and I'll return them promptly to their rightful owners, which is not me. And hurry up, because my mom is here and I don't want her to see them, because (Isabella was really groping for an explanation here) because . . . my . . . mom . . . has . . . a . . . real . . . soft . . . spot . . . for . . . baby . . . animals."

WHAM
WHAM
WHAM

Isabella's mom is really nice and everything, but a soft spot for baby animals? I've seen her pound veal like it owed her money.

Sunday 22

Dear Dumb Diary,

I launched **Operation Beagle Bounce** today and it failed. I blame coffee and dog breeding.

The idea came to me last night, as I watched Stinker gnaw/make-out with Grossnasty, his chew toy.

I really thought this plan could not miss, and here's how it came together:

While my parents were asleep, I put a couple of aspirin bottles and a Kleenex box on Mom's bedside table. I dumped all the coffee beans in the trash and left the empty bag on the counter. Then I changed Dad's alarm clock.

I got dressed for school and picked up my backpack and tiptoed into my parent's room. Then I shook my dad and said, "Dad. Dad. Look at the time! You're late! You're late!" I had to sound really freaked out or it might occur to him that today was Sunday and he didn't have to go to work at all.

The first thing he did was look at my mom, who was still asleep. I pointed at the aspirin and Kleenex. "Don't wake Mom. I don't think she feels well."

Dad jumped into his clothes and came downstairs. I couldn't have him hanging around to maybe wake up Mom. I pointed at the coffeepot: "Out of coffee: Dad, go go go!" Dad ran to his car and hopped in, not noticing that I was right behind him, carrying fat ol' Stinker out to the driveway. He also failed to notice that somebody had tied Grossnasty to the back bumper of his car.

Freaking-out Dad Revving the ENGiNe

Grossnasty

Stinker sees his precious make-out/chew toy.

Dad already drives too fast, but when he thinks he's late for work, he shoots out of the driveway like a rocket. I figured that when Stinker saw Grossnasty taking off, he'd trot behind the car for a while, fussing and wheezing until he eventually got tired and lost. Then somebody would pick him up and return him to us. I figured he'd be back by the end of the week, and by that time, I would have been allowed to submit a picture of a beautiful fawn or swan or something to Isabella's project, because I did not have a pet anymore — my pet had run away.

Oooooh maybe a swan that can do BALLET!

But here's how dog breeding works, I guess. Long ago, people who wanted to invent the beagle looked around for the beagliest animals they could find. And when those two beaglish dogs had puppies, they married those puppies to other super-beagly dogs, until finally, after they did this a jillion times, they got the beagle as we know it today.

How they invented the beagle

I had never really thought about what beagles had been bred *for*. I suppose I thought they were bred to stink and be nuisances, like maybe for homeowners who wanted something to dig up their flower beds but were afraid the neighbors would object to a skunk.

MUNCH

Determination foam →

But it turns out, beagles were bred to chase things, fast things, like foxes and — at this particular moment — chew toys tethered to moving cars.

Stinker took off faster than I had ever seen him move. I could barely hear Dad's tires squealing over the sound of Stinker's toenails scraping on the cement. Stinker caught up to Dad's car quickly and got a good chomp on Grossnasty.

And I learned that there's another thing that beagles were bred to do: **Not Give Up.** Stinker was not going to let go of Grossnasty for anything, not even to avoid being dragged behind a car.

Fortunately (for Stinker), Dad only went a block or so before he had to stop.

For medicine? For gasoline? Nope.

For coffee. Adults' bloodstreams are practically full of it, and my dad is maybe the worst. Since he didn't get it at home, he was willing to be late for work just for a cup of his precious Starbucks. ("Need some latte in my batte," he always says.)

When Dad got out of the car, he noticed Stinker still hanging on to Grossnasty and realized, by looking at a newspaper box outside Starbucks, that it was Sunday.

Dad views smoldering dog

STARBUCK

When Dad got home, he was pretty angry, but I apologized as hard as I could for getting the calendar mixed up, and he just grumped a little, handed me Stinker (who was scruffier and dirtier than ever), and went back to bed.

Like I said, the plan had failed, and it looked like I wasn't going to get rid of Stinker. But then, at that time, I hadn't considered **The Mom Factor.**

Mom sprang her big surprise on us this afternoon.

Remember last week when somebody called and Mom got all excited? It was Miss Bruntford. She had asked Mom for her meat loaf recipe so they could use it to make the **New Improved** school meat loaf.

All the teachers know about my Mom's cooking. Last year, the lemon squares my mom brought for a bake sale caused a dozen kids to lose their hearing for three days.

And one kid says that every thing he eats still tastes lemony.

Mom says she made a little loaf (remember that day when we smelled her cooking but she gave us pizza?) and took it over to Miss Bruntford's. Miss B. tried it, and asked Mom to make a big batch to try on the kids this week at school.

Mom says that Miss Bruntford knows the kids hate the school meat loaf, and she thinks my mom can solve the problem. Mom is so proud of herself that Dad and I were careful not to say anything discouraging. Though I did overhear Dad make a secret call to our insurance agent to see if we were covered if Mom food-poisoned an entire middle school.

So Mom spent the entire day making her meat loaves.

I was in the family room trying not to inhale any more meat loaf odor than I had to when I saw Stinker walk into the kitchen and then walk out. He scratched at the door to go outside. I opened it and he walked down the sidewalk and slowly down the street.

I watched him walk all the way out of sight.

When I looked in the kitchen, I saw what Stinker had seen. Not just a couple of meat loaves, but countless steaming football-shaped meat lumps stacked on every counter.

And I understood: Stinker had done the math. He knows how much leftover meat loaf he is expected to eat from one single meat loaf. The leftovers he thought he was going to have to eat from this batch were just too much to bear.

Mom said that one day I'd appreciate her cooking, and she was right: Today I do.

Stinker has run away from home!

The glorious stink of it all!

Monday 23

Dear Dumb Diary,

That's right! Stinker has run away from home, and Isabella *still* won't let me off the hook. She says the law states that unless the dog is gone forever, or has been given away, or the dog or turtle has been replaced with a different kitten, then it's still my dog, and that's what is going in the project.

I asked her if she meant "puppy" instead of "kitten," and she got all panicky again and said it could be a puppy or a kitten and, besides, those weren't her kittens.

Then she added that I wouldn't need to give her my photos. She already had pictures of me and Stinker that were going to work just fine for her art project.

The shots she probably has →

I wondered if today would be a good day to have a long talk with Mr. Prince, maybe sort out some of these feelings we have for each other, and see if he could get Isabella suspended.

I thought I'd hint at it a little by sculpting Isabella's head in mashed potatoes with a fork stuck in one eye.

SQUORSH
SQUORSH

He didn't notice, though. He wasn't standing by the garbage can today. Mr. Prince was off in a corner talking with Miss Anderson. Probably asking about me. He cares so much.

I think Hudson may have said hi to me today, but I didn't really notice, being so deeply immersed in the romantic fairy tale that is my life, although I still really can't tell if I'm the Princess or the frog. (This fairy-tale report for Evans is going to be tough.)

Also I was pretty hungry and wished that I had eaten Isabella's head instead of throwing it out.

Wait a second. Why did Isabella bring up those kittens again?

Tuesday 24

Dear Dumb Diary,

That was the very first thing I asked Isabella today. I also asked her if the neighbors got their kittens back and if the kittens were happy now and kittens **kittens KITTENS.**

And it was more than Isabella could take. She knows she can't lie to me. It was time for her to give up trying.

I had her and she knew it...

She said it had come to her in a flash in art class that nobody had an uglier pet than I do. Except her. Isabella has a turtle.

So she used her powers of persuasion on her dad to make him take her to the mall to get a kitten, which is one of the all-time cutest animals in the world.

But Isabella says that in as little as a week kitten cuteness starts to fade. And she wanted her pet to be *the* cutest one in the project so that everybody would say that Isabella was the cutest girl in our grade.

So she told her dad that the kitten had run away, and she cried and cried until he took her to get a new one. (As you might recall, Dumb Diary, Isabella's fake crying is unrivaled.)

The replacement kitten also started to lose its cuteness after a week, so she replaced it the same way. She's keeping the extras hidden in her room until the assignment is over.

see?

Kitten cuteness can spoil.

Who knew?

So I had her, right? In my best TV lawyer voice, I pointed out that the **TURTLE** is the real pet and **that's** what has to be in the photo.

Then she got all sinister again and smiled this real horrible smile. "Nope," she said. "Last night, kittens one and two ate the turtle. A shame, really, but it all works out fine in the end."

"But it doesn't work out fine for me. Not for ME!" I said.

And she countered with — get this —"What do you care, with your three boyfriends?"

"Three boyfriends?" I said. **"WHAT** three boyfriends?"

She never answered. She just said that she had even worse pictures of me and Stinker, and if I knew what was good for me, I'd just be quiet about the kittens until the assignment was over.

Isabella has older brothers and is therefore an expert in blackmail.

Other bad pictures Isabella probably has. I'm sure the ones of me are similar.

Wednesday 25

Dear Dumb Diary,

We turned in our art projects today. Isabella was glaring at me and flashed the more awful pictures of me and Stinker, just to keep me in line.

PICTURES TOO HORRIBLE
TO SHOW EVEN IN
MY OWN DIARY

Angeline kept looking at me like she expected me to say something to her, but what did I have to say? I'm either Miss Bruntford or The Beagle. I was done talking.

mine is a
nightmare.
How's
YOUR
Life?

And at lunch today, Pinsetti was jabbering so loud at me, I couldn't hear what Mr. Prince and Miss Anderson were saying, but they were giggling, so I suppose it was about something funny I had said.

The only good thing, I guess, is that Hudson and Angeline were sitting together. I'm grateful that she's taken him off my hands—although as I write this, I can hardly believe I said that. As a matter of fact, I take it back . . .

But I guess that just shows how committed I am to making Mr. Prince wait painfully for me until I am an adult.

Maybe he could carve me out of things while he waits...

me carved out of granite →

me carved out of marble ←

me carved out of a larger sculpture of me ↗

Thursday 26

Dear Dumb Diary,

    Miss Bruntford and Mom's meat loaf are back!

    We all knew this day would come. But what I didn't expect was my mom to show up as well. When your mom shows up at school unexpectedly, you figure that either your house burned down or she read your diary.

    But my mom was just excited to see the kids enjoy her meat loaf. "I told you that you'd appreciate my cooking one day," she said.

TAPPY TAP

TAPPITY

The kids were sitting down with Mom's meat loaf just as Miss Anderson waltzed into the cafeteria and started hanging up the photo assignments. The embarrassment was going to be horrific. I started wondering what my first few therapists were going to be like.

But then a kid screamed as if something had stabbed the inside of his mouth.

It was the meat loaf!

Another kid ran out of the cafeteria covering his mouth, then another. Mom looked distressed, but Miss Bruntford looked absolutely delighted. Way too delighted.

Delighted as if she had planned it this way all along . . .

Then it all became clear to me. As the cafeteria emptied itself of sickened kids, I realized that Miss Bruntford's diabolical scheme was much like Isabella's plan to make herself look better **BY COMPARISON.**

Miss Bruntford's solution was to make the kids eat an **even worse** meat loaf recipe. That way, from that point on, the regular school meat loaf would seem less horrible **BY COMPARISON.**

SCHOOL MEATLOAF

MOM'S MEATLOAF

The cafeteria was empty of kids now, except for me and Angeline — who had not yet taken a bite of her meat loaf. She walked right over to Isabella's project, tore off the picture of Stinker, and replaced it with a different photo she'd pulled out of her pocket.

It was a photo of a beautiful, stunning, immaculately groomed beagle like you'd see on the cover of *American Beagle* magazine.

"It's Stinker," she said.

STINKER, NOW BEAUTIFUL

SMALL, FEMININE HEART ATTACK

"I found him wandering around near our garbage cans last night. He was pretty scruffy-looking, so I washed him up a little. Looked like he had been dragged, if you can believe it.

"I started out with a warm mineral water rinse, then a massage with a diluted baby shampoo. I used a protein-enriched aloe base on his face and head, slowly moving toward a hydrating sheen enhancer along his back. I hit his legs with an herbal, of course, and tipped his tail with a peroxide scrubbing to bring out the white. Then I used a multiplex conditioner with some modifications I made just for the complexities of a beagle's coat, and I trimmed him up, too, using my silver feathering-blade scissors that I bought on eBay. They only manufactured six of these, and five of them have never been outside Hollywood.

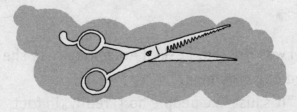

"I figured that this is how he should look in his photo. He's at my house right now. You can pick him up whenever you want."

She handed me the horrible shot of Stinker that she had pulled down. It was an **Extreme Makeover Moment.**

I was floored. I asked Angeline where she learned dog grooming.

"It's just like people hair, really. In fact, my hair is just like Stinker's. Or worse, it's like my mom's."

"My mom is as bad at hair as your mom is at cooking. When I was little, everybody made fun of me. It was pretty awful. I had to learn how to do my hair myself. I checked out books, I studied magazines. I've even examined the hair of the people in front of me at the movies. I learned everything there was to know. If I didn't take care of it myself, it would look just like hers."

I was actually starting to feel bad for Angeline.

"But there was one kid in kindergarten," Angeline continued, "who didn't make fun of me." She pointed to the shot of Miss Bruntford as a kid on our project.

"Miss Bruntford?" I said.

Angeline pulled down the photo and handed it to me. "Yeah, right. I can't believe you let the joke go this long," she said. "I was sure you were going to crack."

REALLY NICE MANICURE

I read the back of the picture. Written in clumsy kindergarten writing, it said, "To Annie from Jamie."

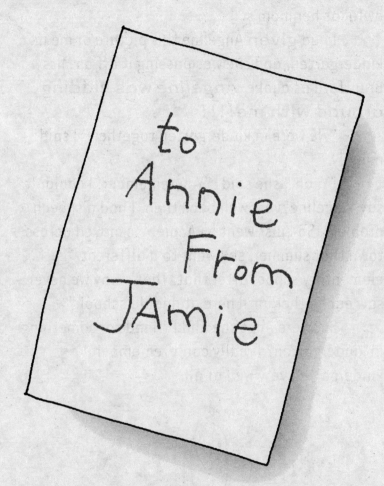

to
Annie
From
Jamie

It was my handwriting. This wasn't a picture of Baby Bruntford. This was a picture of ME!!!!

Suddenly, Angeline's mom **DID** look a little familiar to me. Maybe I **had** seen her before. And way back then, Angeline's hair was, well, just as awful as her mom's.

I had **given** Angeline this picture of me in kindergarten, and she was passing it off as Miss Bruntford as a joke. *Angeline* **was kidding around with me!!!!**

"We were in kindergarten together," I said numbly.

"Yeah," she said. "You remember. I couldn't say 'Angeline' very well back then. I had a speech problem. So I just went by Annie. We moved across town that summer, so I went to a different elementary school after that. That's why we never saw each other until here at middle school."

So, were Angeline and I friends or something in kindergarten? I really can't remember kindergarten very well at all.

Angeline sat back down and started eating the meat loaf.

"You're eating my mom's meat loaf? I asked her, and she pointed with her fork at Mom, who was sitting alone and dejected at a corner table, staring at piles and piles of her rejected steaming meat loaf.

I sat down and started eating it, too. I owed it to Mom. This meat loaf drove Stinker to Angeline, who gave him his makeover, and it drove the kids out of the lunchroom long enough for us to take down the Baby Bruntford photo.

It may be nauseating, but who else's mom's meat loaf can do all that?

Incredibly, even Angeline's gagging noises are kind of pretty.

The bell rang, and as we left the lunchroom, I put the awful picture of Stinker where the Baby Bruntford pic had been on our art project. Mom tried to look like she disapproved, but she was grateful.

It was a busy day, Dumb D, but since my fairy-tale report is due tomorrow, we'd better stop "chatting" now so I can get started on it.

Miss Bruntford

Then   **Now**

it made me wish that Stinker was even uglier.

Friday 27

Dear Dumb Diary,

Mr. Evans made me give my report first today, like he always does. I told him I had done my report on a few different fairy tales.

First, I talked about the witch in *Snow White*, and how she used a poison apple to make herself look better, but she could have just as easily used a poison meat loaf. Fairy tales remind us that there really are wicked, mean people walking around.

But fairy tales are short, and they leave out certain things, like, who do you think had to wash Rapunzel's hair after the Prince got his muddy boots all over it? That's right: Rapunzel did.

And you may think that these Princesses have it easy, but some of them started out as Ugly Ducklings, and some of the swans may actually end up as Ugly Ducklings. Fairies can do that to a swan, you know.

The ugly duckling that grew into an uglier duck.

And then I looked right at Isabella as I finished up my report, and I said that Hansel and Gretel made a mistake with the bread crumbs. They almost got eaten up because of it, but they stuck together and they got out of the woods in one piece. And Isabella knew what I meant.

But I had to admit, I'm not sure I ever really figured out *The Frog Prince.*

Mr. Evans throbbed only a little, which means I got a B. Isabella and I made up at lunch, which was good, since it looks like Mr. Prince is gone forever, now that Miss Bruntford is back. (I could just die!) I'm certain he'll write me when he settles in at his next job.

I admitted to Isabella that her kitten was the cutest pet in the photos, and she said that Stinker had never looked better.

I gotta admit- Isabella is awfully clever

I told her about Angeline. Isabella doesn't believe Angeline and I ever knew each other in kindergarten. Except last night after my report, I dug through my old school stuff and I found a picture. The writing on the back was unreadable, but I really think this may be Angeline.

FRONT
I think it's kindergarten Angeline!

Here's what she wrote on the BACK →

I told Angeline I was coming over to get Stinker tomorrow, and she said she'd do my hair if I wanted her to.

Think about it: **This is like having Einstein offer to help you with your math homework.**

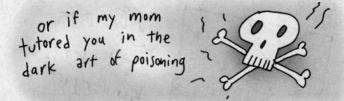

or if my mom tutored you in the dark art of poisoning

OR if Mr. Prince taught how to be all totally handsome

(C Y J D ?)

HYUK HYUK HYUK

or if any parent anywhere gave lessons on embarrassing kids.

Saturday 28

Dear Dumb Diary,

So I taped that kindergarten picture of Angeline into my diary and took it over to her house to ask if it was really her. She said it was, and was all excited that I keep a diary because she says she does, too.

I think I was surprised that Angeline's house was NOT full of the fanciful pink unicorns you would probably expect.

But then she asked if she could read it.

Awkward, right? Since on one or two occasions, I may have written something unpleasant about Angeline, and I **REALLY** wanted her to fix my hair. So I said I'd let her read the love poems that Mr. Prince had sent me, but that was it.

Angeline looked a little startled, and read the first one and smiled. Then she read the second one and grinned.

"These aren't from Mr. Prince," she said.

"What makes you say that?" I asked, getting angry, but not angry enough to walk away from a hair makeover.

"I get a **lot** of notes, Jamie. I can identify

the handwriting of every boy in the school. These were written by Mike Pinsetti. See? **M.P.** doesn't stand for **Mr. Prince**, it stands for **Mike Pinsetti**."

For a moment, I thought I could taste yesterday's meat loaf.

"See, Pinsetti's nicknaming skill has two sides. He's also a good poet. He's just good with words in general."

Yup, it was yesterday's meat loaf all right.

"Also, Mr. Prince is dating Miss Anderson. At first, I'm sure he probably thought she was a bit old for him, but that picture of her in our art project may have changed his mind."

Curse those who can pose adorably!

Miss Anderson

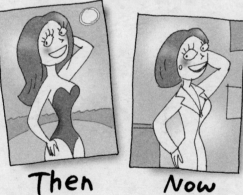

Then   Now

"And by the way, Jamie, if you really do think that a teacher or any old guy has sent you a poem like this, he totally belongs in Gross Guy Prison. You're in **middle school.** Seriously. You should know better."

GROSS GUY PRISON

WELCOME CREEPS

I didn't know what to say. Angeline was right. I weakly flipped to the third poem and, as Angeline read it, I saw her face totally change.

"Take your dog and go," she said. Just like that.

"Go?" I said.

"Go. No cutting. No styling. No highlighting. No moisturizing. No silkifying. No conditioning, and definitely **NO ZONE SHAMPOOING!**" She handed me Stinker and ushered us out the door, and I don't know which one of us was more upset about leaving.

"Angeline, why?" I said. "What did I do?"

"The poem," she said. "The lousy one. That's **Hudson's** handwriting. Do you honestly think I'm going to fix your hair and help you win Hudson back?"

And she slammed the door.

So there **IS** such a thing as **Zone Shampooing!** Can you imagine what I could have become?

Sunday 29

Dear Dumb Diary,

    I spoke to Isabella on the phone this morning and she says that Angeline withholding her hair technology goes to show that maybe I **was** right before: Pretty Maidens **ARE** the cause of all the troubles in fairy tales. That, and jealousy.

Isabella told me that the reason she had gone through with the photo assignment is that she was jealous of me. Weeks ago, when I attempted my own version of Zone Shampooing on Hudson and was led away by Mr. Evans, I hadn't seen Hudson's reaction. Isabella saw **pure love** squirting out of Hudson's ears. Zone Shampooing had worked.

But not because I had fragranced him. Only Angeline could have taught me the right way to do that. But because Hudson thought I was **funny**.

Then when Isabella saw Pinsetti squirt pure love out of his ears, too, *and* she thought Mr. Prince was sending me poems, she couldn't help herself. Isabella turned into **The Evil Queen of Pure Jealous Revenge.**

After Isabella and I hung up, I tried to figure out the whole Frog Prince thing.

I was the frog for Mr. Prince, but he was the Prince for Miss Anderson. I was the frog for Hudson, then the Princess, and then the frog again. So it looks like I'm both the Princess *and* the frog.

Later on, the doorbell rang, and I found a letter on my front porch. I opened it and found this poem inside:

YOUR EYES

I saw your picture on the wall,
It seemed to hypnotize.
I saw the kind and gentle heart
Behind your big brown eyes.

m.p.

And then I knew that I really was the Princess. I was the Princess for Mike Pinsetti. Sure, it's only Pinsetti, but at least **I'M TOTALLY THE PRINCESS.**

But then I read the poem again. I don't have
brown eyes. Nobody in my family has brown eyes.

When I flipped the envelope over, I saw it was addressed to Stinker. I guess the work Angeline did on Stinker moved Pinsetti to write a poem. Considering how ugly that little beagle began, I suppose he is the only **real** Frog Prince in this whole dumb fairy tale. And if I have to give up my throne to somebody he probably deserves it most of all.

Thanks for listening, Dumb Diary.

Jamie Kelly

About Jim Benton

Jim Benton is not a middle-school girl, but do not hold that against him. He has managed to make a living out of being funny, anyway.

He is the creator of many licensed properties, some for big kids, some for little kids, and some for grown-ups who, frankly, are probably behaving like little kids.

You may already know his properties: It's Happy Bunny™ or Just Jimmy™, and you are about to get to know Dear Dumb Diary.

He's created a kids' TV series, designed clothing, and written books.

Jim Benton lives in Michigan with his spectacular wife and kids. They do not have a dog, and they especially do not have a vengeful beagle. This is his first series for Scholastic.

Jamie Kelly has no idea that Jim Benton, or you, or anybody is reading her diaries.

Don't Miss the next
Dear Dumb Diary

4: NEVER DO ANYTHING, EVER

Dear Dumb Diary,

Isabella said that she got the information about this charity online and I could help her collect for it if I wanted to, so as we made the rounds for the clothes, we also picked up a few bucks here and there for the Juvenile Optometry Federation.

Hooray! Now I have a charity to work for. In your face, Angeline — now I'm as gentle and sweet as you, you pig!!